"I FEEL RELAXED WITH YOU," JIM SAID GENTLY.

"Thank you," Mel responded guardedly.

"I hope you don't think I'm giving you a line."

She smiled weakly. "What made you say that?"

He raised his eyes to hers. "It's just that I know how you might think that. Don't get me wrong, it has nothing to do with me. I mean personally. But when people are on a ship, everything seems more romantic. At least, many of the passengers think so."

Was he trying to tell her not to make more of his words than was intended? "Don't worry. I wouldn't dream of letting the moonlight dazzle my judgment."

"Well, I'm glad to hear that, since most people have the wrong idea about my position as captain."

"You don't owe me any explanations."

"That's where you're wrong. I want to get to know you and I want to make sure you understand me."

"Well, Captain, I'm flattered, but the cruise will be over soon and we'll never see each other again, so why don't we just enjoy each other for the time being." With that, she picked up her wrap and left the dining room.

CANDLELIGHT ECSTASY CLASSIC ROMANCES

CANDLELIGHT ECSTASY ROMANCES®

THE CAPTAIN'S SEDUCTION

Joan Grove

A CANDLELIGHT ECSTASY ROMANCE®

Published by
Dell Publishing Co., Inc.
1 Dag Hammarskjold Plaza
New York, New York 10017

Dell ® TM 681510, Dell Publishing Co., Inc.

Candlelight Ecstasy Romance®, 1,203,540, is a registered trademark of Dell Publishing Co., Inc., New York, New York.

ISBN: 0-440-10962-0

Printed in the United States of America

July 1987

10 9 8 7 6 5 4 3 2 1

WFH

Special thanks to ex-Captain Hugh Stephens for his help, and to Lydia and Nancy for their faith and guidance.

To Our Readers:

We have been delighted with your enthusiastic response to Candlelight Ecstasy Romances®, and we thank you for the interest you have shown in this exciting series.

In the upcoming months we will continue to present the distinctive sensuous love stories you have come to expect only from Ecstasy. We look forward to bringing you many more books from your favorite authors and also the very finest work from new authors of contemporary romantic fiction.

As always, we are striving to present the unique, absorbing love stories that you enjoy most—books that are more than ordinary romance. Your suggestions and comments are always welcome. Please write to us at the address below.

Sincerely,

The Editors
Candlelight Romances
1 Dag Hammarskjold Plaza
New York, New York 10017

THE CAPTAIN'S
SEDUCTION

CHAPTER ONE

What a spectacular sight! Melanie Ford exclaimed silently as her hazel eyes took in every detail of the incredibly impressive white, sleek, and unbelievably large ship.

Excitement surged through her as she thought about her upcoming voyage, but disbelief suddenly softened her reaction. Her sedentary life as a sociology teacher and small-town resident made Mel feel that someone should pinch her to prove that the anticipation of the cruise had become a mind-boggling reality. Not only would this be Mel's first cruise, but also her first trip alone. She would have preferred the company of a friend, and without one, she was a little concerned about what lay ahead. But the adventurous side of her personality, which had been suppressed for so long, would not be discouraged, and she looked forward eagerly to the alluring possibilities of the jaunt.

The weight of her suitcase finally registered, and Mel immediately set it down. Wondering what time they would board, she glanced anxiously at her watch and then turned to note the milling crowd. Fellow passengers were being hugged by relatives or loved ones. A smile brightened her face until a sharp wave of envy engulfed her as she suddenly wished that someone were seeing her off. But her hometown was a long way from Florida, and not one of her friends could be there. Her best friend, Helen, who had wanted to join her, couldn't because of a deadline at work. Suddenly feeling so alone, last-minute doubts flooded her mind. She hoped she'd still be thankful for Helen's part in arranging the trip when the cruise was over. But she reassured herself the trip was for only a few days, and she was determined to make the best of it.

As some of the passengers headed toward the ship, Mel grabbed her suitcase, took one last look at the ground around her, squared her shoulders, and moved toward the gangplank. Once she reached the ramp, she glanced up. Tall, good-looking officers in their smart blue uniforms stood in a line, waiting to welcome the passengers aboard.

Her step faltered as her friends' words of caution flashed through her head. The officers with their eager eyes suddenly looked as if they were ready to pounce on the first woman they saw, she thought warily. There was no denying their overwhelming masculine appeal, and she could easily understand how lonely, vulnerable women could fall prey to these handsome devils. An image of lambs being led to slaughter up a gangplank came instantly to mind, and Mel checked the grimace that tugged at the corners of her mouth. She had promised herself to be objective, regardless of the stories she'd heard, and she was going to try her darnedest to keep her word. She forced a smile as she continued up the walk and acknowledged the officers' greetings.

When she reached the top, one of the men quickly

offered, "Allow me," took her suitcase, and whisked her off to the registrar.

Checking in was speedy enough, and Mel soon found herself alone in her cabin. She took in the small room with its compact, wooden furniture, plaid curtains, and matching bedspread. A bottle of red wine, two glasses, and a small bouquet rested on a table near the bed. *Nice touch*, she thought as she raised the strap of her purse off her shoulder and laid it next to the flowers. The inviting porthole caught her attention, and Mel followed her impulse to inspect the view. As she peered through the round glass, her spirits rose when she beheld the sparkling, fathomless water.

Abruptly she turned away and walked over to her suitcase, and promptly unpacked. Feeling tired from her flight from Pittsburgh, she flopped onto the bed and stretched out, hoping to take a nap. Minutes passed, and she couldn't sleep. Her body was willing, but her mind was awhirl with thoughts of the events which led up to her decision to take the cruise.

Her life in Pittsburgh had become too routine, and she wanted a change. A cruise seemed like the perfect answer, but after talking to some of her friends who had taken cruises, doubts flooded her mind. Even though her girlfriends still urged her to go, they didn't fail to warn her that the ship's officers were often pros at chasing women and lovemaking.

Confused, Mel discussed the trip with Helen, who was an editor for a local magazine. After telling Helen the stories she had heard about how some women passengers had been taken advantage of, Helen suggested that the stories would be great material for an article. Helen pointed out that Mel, with her sociology background and naïveté about cruises, should be able to give an interesting slant on a story about a woman taking a cruise alone. Hesitant of the offer, she pointed out that she wasn't a good writer, but Helen reassured her that she would work with Mel on the story. Helen also stated that if the article were bought, Mel could get the cost of the cruise included in her fee and have a paid summer vacation. Well, that was a deal that she couldn't refuse. Helen was quite pleased, but concerned about Mel's ability to handle the ship's officers' advances. Mel had reassured her that forewarned was forearmed. So, Mel had booked a cruise to the Virgin Islands, and the rest was history.

Suddenly remembering that she wanted to take a Dramamine pill to ward off any seasickness, Mel was pulled out of her thoughts. Slowly bringing herself up to a sitting position, she reached for her purse and opened it, taking out the bottle of pills and a miniature tape recorder. She pressed the recording button and spoke, "Melanie Ford here. Just arrived aboard ship. Unbelievable experience—more than words can describe. The ship is elegant. The officers extremely handsome. Can easily understand their appeal."

She snapped off the machine, and slipped it back into her bag. Then she quickly scanned the trip's itinerary given to her by the registrar. Surprised, she noted a boat and safety drill, which was on the top of the list, and the time given. She glanced at her watch and realized that she had only a few minutes to make it.

She immediately slipped out of her tailored linen suit, and into a red polo shirt and white slacks. Opening the bottle of Dramamine, she headed for the bathroom for a glass of water and swallowed a pill. She grabbed her purse and on her way to the door caught her reflection in the floor-length mirror. Her makeup was okay, but the humidity of Fort Lauderdale had made a limp mess out of her fine shoulder-length auburn hair. Mel shrugged. She didn't have time to curl it, so it would just have to do. Slamming the door behind her, she hurried toward the purser's office to get directions for the room indicated for the drill.

After getting the information, she strolled out of the office, made a left, and continued down a long corridor until she reached the entrance of the room. She paused and looked in at the empty room except for two officers.

"Excuse me," she said loudly, thinking she had found the wrong room.

The officers turned to face her. Immediately sensing her confusion, one of the officers announced, "The passengers have been moved to the boat deck. Go out the door to the left and go above to your right."

She nodded her thanks and took off. Being late was not easy for her to take, especially since she was a high-school teacher, and promptness was an integral part of her personality.

Finding the steps, she took them as fast as her legs would carry her. As she reached the top, she was out of breath. Pushing the door in front of her, she stepped out onto the deck.

To her chagrin, the drill had already begun and crew members were handing out life jackets. Quickly she found an opening toward the forward life boats and reached for an offered vest. Trying to appear as if she knew what she was doing, she immediately slipped it on. Attempting to pull the strap across her, she realized it was twisted and as she straightened it, she suddenly felt eyes upon her, and her head jerked up. But everyone around her was busy with his own jacket. She thought she must have been wrong, but the feeling of being watched remained.

Trusting herself, she looked around again, and then, as if pulled by some magical cord, her eyes focused on the wing of the bridge. Sure enough, a tall man in uniform was staring down at her. By his dress, white cap, and four gold stripes on his jacket sleeve, she was certain that he was the captain. She couldn't make out the exact features of his face, but his appearance was so compelling that he reminded her of a mighty Viking with his red hair and strong, large frame.

A strange, undefinable feeling flashed through her. She struggled to find the words to explain her reaction. Vulnerable, weakened, uncomfortable, were as close as she could come. Too shaken to look away, her eyes were held locked, staring up at him. Suddenly without warning, she witnessed the most magnetic grin ever. His pearly whites would stand out anywhere. Without thinking, her inviting lips smiled in return. From some unknown source, she found the strength to pull away from his intense stare and glanced down at her vest, which now felt like a dead weight.

Helen's words of caution came sharply to mind, and Mel already seriously doubted her ability to withstand the advances of one particular ship's officer. She suddenly wished that Helen were there with her; Helen would surely know how to handle this.

Mel stared blankly down at the strings on her vest and tried to tie them. But she was still bothered by her strong response to the stranger, and her hand trembled. She tried to push her feelings aside and to concentrate on the life jacket, but she felt all thumbs. She sighed deeply and wondered how she could gracefully slip off the deck without the big guy noticing.

"Need some help?" The man's voice jerked her out of her reverie, and Mel looked up. A pleasant-looking officer smiled down at her.

Before she had a chance to answer him, he went on "The captain asked me to see if you needed any assistance in tying your life jacket. Knots in the ties can be very dangerous, especially if you have to get out of your jacket in a hurry. Just tie it as you would your shoe strings."

"Thanks, I'll keep that in mind," she answered quickly, wishing to be left alone, and just to show him how capable she was, she began to tie the strings.

"Good," he declared with a nod of approval, and immediately moved on to another passenger.

Mel glanced up at the bridge, but her Viking was gone. So he had sent his officer to help her. Did she look like a helpless female, or had she just been introduced to the captain? Neither explanation sat very well with her. Regardless of how vulnerable she had felt toward the man, she wouldn't be an easy mark. And if he had any inkling that she was, he had another think coming!

Not wanting her evening to be spoiled, she dismissed the irritation that was building and glanced down at her vest. She swiftly completed the task of tying the strings and turned her attention to the drill instructor.

"In case of emergency, *don't* panic. Obey instructions from the crew. Proceed slowly and don't run," the officer stated. "If there aren't any further questions and life jackets have been successfully fastened, please return the jackets to the crew. Thank you and have a pleasant cruise."

A round of applause thundered throughout the room. Noting that her fellow passengers were now taking off their jackets and returning them to crew members, she began to untie hers. But in her careless attempt to tie the strings, they were knotted. Darn! she thought with annoyance, and pulled at the strings.

"Looks like you've got a problem there, lady." The deep voice startled her. Mel looked up and her eyes focused on a large Adam's apple protruding from a thick, reddish neck. Tension settled between her shoulder blades as her eyes slowly traveled up the strong chin and into the same good-looking man's face who had been up on the bridge. A faintly amused glint sparkled in his gorgeous blue eyes. He was towering over her, and Mel found herself weaving backward.

Fighting to regain her composure, she quickly mumbled, "I'm fine, thank you."

"I agree that you're fine, but *can* you get out of your life jacket?" he inquired with a mischievous grin.

"Positive," she almost snapped.

Her defenses were up, and she wanted to make sure the man didn't get the wrong idea. Determined to appear sophisticated, she glanced down at the knot and gave the string a sharp yank. To her dismay, she almost ripped the string from the vest.

"I guess I don't know my own strength," she said weakly with a nervous laugh.

How embarrassing, she thought as she glanced un-

18

easily down at the floor. Perhaps she could find a crack in the deck to wiggle into.

"Life jackets aren't made the way they used to be, and neither are women, for that matter," he said with a sunny smile.

She wanted to ask what he meant by that remark, but didn't, afraid that her voice would give away the shakiness she felt being near him.

"You need a man to show you how it's done," he said confidently, taking matters into his own hands and expertly separating the ties.

"You certainly take over!" she blurted out, defensively.

Her cheeks instantly grew hot, and she wondered what on earth had caused her to be so direct.

"It's my job to keep everybody happy," he said with such sudden humbleness that Mel eyed him suspiciously.

She wondered if there was a double meaning here, and whether he was really being helpful, or whether it was only a part of his line. But she decided that perhaps she was being too skeptical and smiled politely.

"Well, thanks for your help," she stated, hoping that would be the end of their conversation.

"Did you see how I did it?" he asked with challenging eyes.

"Oh, yes, of course, I did," she retorted, and added a confident smile to convince him.

Not wanting a repeat performance, she made sure that he kept his distance. Truthfully, she really had no recollection of the incident at all. The only thing she recalled was the nice smell of his lime aftershave when he bent close to her.

"I want to make sure that you enjoy your cruise," he said sincerely.

"Thank you."

"Are you traveling alone?" he inquired.

"Yes."

"Well, I don't want you to get lonely," he said in a friendly way.

"I'm sure I won't," she anwered quickly.

"One never knows. After a few nights on the water, it has a strange effect on some people, makes them do things that normally they wouldn't do," he replied with a mysterious edge to his voice.

She wondered what the captain was suggesting as she insisted, "I'm positive, I'll be all right."

"I just want you to know that I'm the captain and if there's anything you want, I'll see to it that you get it," he offered graciously.

Boy, this man was too much, she thought, pulling rank for his own personal needs!

"Do you have any questions?" he asked abruptly, pulling her out of her thoughts.

"About what?" she asked, not knowing what he'd say next.

"In case of fire . . ."

"Oh, no, I don't," she interrupted.

"Then I'm sure you can take care of yourself," he stated with a nod.

"I can, thank you."

"Well, if you get lonely or need anything, I'm Jim O'Dowd," he announced, and offered his hand.

As she shook his hand, she wondered if all she had to do was whistle.

His large, manly hand had a strong grip, and Mel

20

figured he'd be great at arm wrestling and would no doubt always win. He held her hand a bit longer than she had anticipated. When he did release his grasp, he smiled at her, and their eyes met and held. An awkwardness came over her as she looked away.

Suddenly remembering that she still had her jacket on, she saw her out and took it. Looking back at the captain, she quickly said, "Thanks again. Excuse me."

She caught a surprised look in his eyes before she turned and fled. For some strange reason, Mel felt as though she had escaped with her life.

Taking off her jacket, she handed it to one of the crew and then found a safe spot alongside a middle-aged couple to hear instructions for the evening's events. But Mel couldn't concentrate on what was being said. All she could think about was her reaction to the captain.

"Hi." A tap on her shoulder made Mel turn and stare into the face of a young officer.

"Sorry to startle you, but I've been watching you and felt you needed some company," he announced in a friendly way.

"No, I don't," she replied, not believing the man's audacity.

"This is your first cruise, isn't it?" he inquired, knowingly.

"Yes, it is," she answered flatly, suddenly wishing that she knew what the young man was up to.

"How about getting together later?" he asked with a grin.

Perhaps she was about to find out, she reasoned sarcastically. "Just what do you have in mind?" she asked, wanting to make certain of his intention, so as not to jump to the wrong conclusion.

"I thought maybe we could do some dancing and have some laughs," he replied eagerly. "You're a very pretty lady, and I think we could have a good time," he went on with his spiel, and instantly Mel was reminded of a used-car salesman.

Mel squinted her eyes. He had emphasized the word "good" a little too much. "I'm very tired, and I think I'll pass," she stated as politely as possible.

"Well, the night's early. Take a nap, and we can meet later," he urged.

Didn't the guy know when to take "no" for an answer? "No, that's not possible," she stated firmly.

"I just want to make certain you have fun," he stated in a cocky way.

"Don't give it a second thought, because I intend to," she retorted.

"Well, if there's anything you need . . ."

"Just let you know," she broke in.

"Exactly," he came back eagerly, not in the least bit put off by her sarcasm.

Gimme a break! she thought, and snapped, "I'll be sure to let you know. Now, if you don't mind, I'd like to get back to my cabin."

"I saw you talking to the captain," he said, disregarding her words.

"Yes?"

"He has all the luck, that guy," he said with deep appreciation.

She assumed that he was implying that the captain had his way with the women, and she retorted wearily, "I'm sure he has."

Mel should have packed a club to beat these guys off with, she thought with annoyance.

Giving an offhanded salute to another officer, he stated abruptly, "Sorry, got to go. But I'm sure I'll see you later," he added in a knowing way.

Not if she could help it, she silently answered as she watched the young man's exit.

She shook her head in disbelief. The ship had barely left port, and two officers had already brazenly approached her. But Mel's courage wasn't daunted. Her dander was up, making her all the more determined to resist all advances. She wasn't a toy to be played with, and they'd soon find that out.

Her article came sharply to mind. Mel looked carefully around to make certain that no one was watching her. Convinced they weren't, she opened her bag and took out her tape recorder. She hesitated, knowing she should wait until she got back to her cabin. But afraid that she might forget something, she pushed the record button and began, "Boat barely out of port and have been hit on by two good-looking officers. One extremely striking hunk was the captain. Definite sex appeal. If not on guard, could easily fall under his spell. Other one, younger and more aggressive, not as interesting."

Suddenly she caught sight of the tall captain headed in her direction. She quickly snapped off the machine and dropped it back into her purse. She turned sharply on her heel, walked off the deck, and headed toward her cabin, still on too shaky ground to want to encounter the unsettling man again. Not until she had showered and rested would she be able to deal with that man with any ounce of sanity.

Later that evening, Mel stood in line, waiting to be announced to the captain and his chief officers. The men had changed into their white, spiffy uniforms and looked very handsome. For the second time that day Mel felt very alone and seriously doubted her decision to take the cruise. She was dressed in a strapless blue formal gown, and, instead of feeling attractive, she felt awkward, out of place. Everywhere she looked, everyone was with someone. She suddenly felt a bit like the ugly stepsister nobody wanted to invite to the ball.

As she neared the reception line, she squared her shoulders and forced a smile upon her face. She didn't want anyone to know how vulnerable she was. No, that wouldn't do, she warned herself.

"Miss Melanie Ford," the purser announced, and Mel instantly tensed. She had firmly instructed the purser that she wanted her title to be Ms., and now all the officers knew that she was single. A frown betrayed her feelings as she shook the large white-gloved hands that were extended to her.

Finally, she reached the captain. "Nice to see you again, Miss Ford," he offered warmly.

"Thank you," she said politely, and was strangely thankful to see one familiar face.

"I hope you don't mind my saying so, but you certainly look very lovely tonight," he declared, his eyes showing his appreciation.

"Thank you again," she replied as a small smile twitched at the corners of her lips. She quickly moved away.

He certainly was a silver-tongued devil! And the funny part was that she did suddenly feel very lovely.

Mel took her seat next to the same middle-aged couple she had sat next to after the drill. She sipped champagne as she listened to Peg and Joe Harper's many stories of previous cruises and couldn't help be pleasantly surprised at how perfect everything was. The whole setting, from the candlelit dinner to the flowers, was extemely romantic, and Mel found herself happy for the first time in a long while. There was excitement in the air, and she felt a part of it.

Her eyes wandered every once in a while across to the captain seated at the next table. She wondered if he was married, noting how his head was bent close to a stunning blonde in what seemed to be a very intimate conversation. As they spoke, the blonde would lightly caress his hand and he in turn would squeeze her fingers gently. She had hoped that he was different from the officers she'd heard stories about, but by the look of the things, he probably was just like any other male on the make. This disappointed her, but she realized that it was better for her to see him in action now, so she wouldn't be taken in by him later. Besides, she reasoned, he could always argue that it was a part of his duty to socialize and to keep the passengers happy.

While the melodious music played and after she'd had coffee and dessert, Mel turned her eyes in the direction of the band and immediately spotted the captain dancing with a tall brunette in a tight-fitting gold dress. He held her so close that the woman looked as if she were having trouble breathing. The guy certainly got around, she mused as she took a large bite of her chocolate mousse. The brunette suddenly threw back her head and laughed, with her hands clasped around the back of his head and the captain automatically

25

pulled her in tighter to him again. How very cozy, she thought irritably, immediately looking away and proceeding to polish off her dessert. Finally, feeling stuffed to the gills, she leaned back in her chair.

"This is the way to live," she murmured to the silver-haired Peg sitting next to her.

"That's what we decided," Peg retorted, smiling proudly at her husband.

He laughed and asked, "How about a dance, honey?"

Peg smiled again, and Mel thought she even detected a slight blush.

"Will you excuse us?" Peg asked politely.

"Of course, have a good time," Mel replied, and smiled as she watched the couple walk, hand in hand, onto the dance floor.

How lovely, she thought, to grow old with the man you loved. So many of her friends' marriages had ended in divorce, which saddened her and had made her more determined not to rush into marriage. Even if it took a long time, she would wait for the perfect man for her. She was a romantic and would remain one until someone convinced her otherwise.

As her eyes took in the couple dancing, she noted their happiness, which gave her renewed hope in love.

She suddenly wondered where the captain was and glanced around the group. But the handsome man was nowhere in sight, and remembering the young officer's words, she wondered whether the captain hadn't again gotten lucky.

The words "What is a beautiful woman like yourself doing, sitting by herself?" interrupted her thoughts, and she turned to find Captain O'Dowd, with expectant eyes, staring down at her.

Against her will, she smiled. She couldn't help it; he just had that effect on her. "Having a good time, that's what," she said cheerfully, and noticed the cup of coffee resting in his large hand.

"Would you care to dance?" he asked, setting his cup on the table.

By his action, it was obvious that the captain expected her to accept his offer, but he was in for a letdown. Mel instinctively knew that being in his arms would stretch her willpower to the limit, and besides she had too much pride to be thought of as another one of his easy conquests.

"No, thank you," she returned politely.

Not daunted in the least, he plopped down in the chair next to her and asked, "Is this your first cruise?"

If one more person asked that question, she'd scream. "Yes, it is. Does it show?"

"A little. Why do you ask?" he asked with keen interest.

"It's just that you're the second person who's asked me that."

"Not very original of me," he said with a doubtful look in his eyes.

"No, that's not what I meant . . ."

"It's okay, I can take it. Conversation with lovely women has never been my forte," he confessed, and then took a sip of his coffee.

By the way he had maneuvered the blonde and the brunette, she had to agree, *talking* definitely wasn't his strong point.

"I'm sure you manage quite well," she came back, tongue in cheek.

"You wouldn't believe it, but I am quite shy," he said, looking innocently into her eyes.

Oh, boy, gimme a break—not the little boy routine, she silently fumed. "No, I never would have thought that," she said flatly, not wanting to encourage the subject.

"You work?"

She stared at him stubbornly. Now he was getting personal, and she didn't want the operator to have anything on her. But not knowing how to avoid his question without being rude, she decided to make him work for his answers.

"Yes," she said curtly.

"What do you do?" he asked, indifferent to her reluctance to talk.

For someone who was shy, he made up for it in the nosy department, she thought somewhat sarcastically.

"I'm a teacher, a high-school teacher," she admitted.

A grin curled up the corners of his mouth.

"Does something amuse you?" she inquired immediately.

He raised his hand and explained, "I instantly knew there was something I liked about you. Not only are you a very attractive lady, but a very intelligent one too."

Mel looked at him in disbelief. Why should he even think about whether she was smart? It was bad enough that he had to come on to her, but couldn't he be a little less obvious?

"That *was* a compliment," he drawled.

"Thanks for the compliment," she said a little coolly.

"I like to read, too," he stated proudly with a charming smile that could have melted her heart.

But Mel was on guard; the captain wasn't about to steal her affection. "That's a good habit to get into," she returned pleasantly.

"Yes, I like mysteries the best," he offered.

"I do too."

His big blue eyes brightened as he exclaimed, "We have something in common."

"Yes, we do, Captain O'Dowd."

"Please call me Jim," he said quietly.

Mel smiled as she took in his red curly hair. One strand mischievously fell over his forehead. He was adorable, like a big teddy bear. More like a grizzly bear, she cautioned, annoyed with herself for being so easily taken in, even briefly, by this man.

"Where are you from?" he suddenly asked.

"Adamsville, a small town outside of Pittsburgh," she answered without thinking.

"I have a good friend in Pittsburgh," he exclaimed.

She wondered of which sex, but replied, sweetly, "That's nice."

Abruptly he stood up. She stared up at him questioningly.

"Excuse me, I've taken up enough of your time," he explained. "I hope to see you in the morning."

Mel nodded.

"Pleasant dreams," he said in a quiet tone, then turned and walked away.

Mel's eyes followed the man's exit. His broad shoulders fit his white jacket like a glove, and his stroll depicted a confident man who was in control and knew where he was going as he joined a beautiful redhead at another table.

She sighed deeply. What made the guy think that she was going to bed early? Her eyes quickly scanned the room for any available men, but the women outnumbered the men five to one, excluding the crew, of course. No wonder the officers could have a field day with lonely women. She frowned. She might as well call it a day.

She stood, and out of the corner of her eye she caught sight of a white-uniformed man moving quickly toward her. By his smug grin and the hungry look in his eyes, Mel easily identified the young officer. Mel took off, and in her haste caught her heel in the hem of her gown and almost went sailing across the room. Luckily she grabbed a chair and managed to right herself. With every ounce of her remaining dignity, she straightened her shoulders and walked swiftly out of the room.

Not until she was in her room was Mel able to laugh at herself. She couldn't believe what an idiot she had been. She hoped that the captain hadn't witnessed her spectacle. The captain. He certainly was a handsome devil! The kind of man that she'd always fantasized about meeting. He was handsome, intelligent, and very considerate. But it was a shame that he was such a womanizer. Why would such an attractive and seemingly intelligent man have to stoop to such tactics? Mel sighed deeply and decided that even if she lived to be a hundred, she'd never have the answer to that one.

The good-looking man had to be put out of her thoughts—she had work to do. She quickly slipped out of her gown and into her nightshirt. Taking out a legal pad, she made notes of the pertinent facts of the day, including all the descriptions of the officers, the passengers, the different rooms, and everything she could think of, right down to her chocolate mousse. As she looked over all the information, she realized that she might soon have enough data to fill a whole book.

Finally, her hand became cramped, and she set her pad and pencil on the small table next to her bed. She switched off the lamp and crawled under the sheet. Closing her eyes, she hoped to sleep, but unfortunately she was suddenly disturbed. Her body tingled at the mere thought of Jim. Never before in her life had she ever been so excited by one man. His whole being seemed to invade her very essence. She didn't know how that was possible, especially since she hardly knew the man. He hadn't even kissed her or touched her. For a practical, logical woman these new feelings were very difficult to deal with and Mel lay there wide-eyed, feeling suddenly that life wasn't very fair. She grabbed her pillow and hugged it to her. Here she was, so attracted to a man and she wouldn't do anything about it, because he was the wrong man. A Casanova who lived by his charm and good looks to seduce women. No, life wasn't fair, she groaned. She didn't even know what he thought of her, and the worst part of it was that even if he would tell her that he was interested in her, she would, no doubt, question his motives.

Saddened, Mel sat up in bed and slowly swung her legs over the side. She walked to the porthole and stared out at the water. A light flashed out in the distance. She shivered, feeling instantly lonely. She wondered what Jim was doing right now. If he was in bed, and if he was alone.

Jim sat fully dressed, a drink in his hand with his legs stretched out on his bed. A crack had dented his armor, and he didn't like it at all. He thought he was beyond being taken in by a pretty face and lovely eyes. He had been on enough cruises to feel that he was immune to having special feelings for any of the women passengers. Not that women hadn't tried to seduce him, they had, and it had always made him uncomfortable. Especially when they were wealthy, bored married women who felt that he was there to amuse them. At times, he was attracted to some of the passengers, but his social life was pretty active off the ship. So he didn't need to mix business with pleasure. That was until Miss Ford came waltzing across his boat deck.

Melanie. There was something so gentle and sensitive about her that brought out his natural instinct to protect her. It wasn't anything that she did. She certainly seemed confident enough. It was more of an instinctual reaction. He was operating on some unknown force from deep inside that had responded to this beautiful woman. And he truly felt that she was different from any other woman he had ever met. Call it chemistry or sex appeal, it didn't matter what name was given to the strong pull he felt toward her; it was the first real emotion he had experienced in a long time. And it scared him.

It didn't make sense. He raised his glass to his lips and swallowed the soothing Scotch. The worst yet was that he knew nothing about her, except that she was a schoolteacher—and could be a married schoolteacher at that. Just because she'd been introduced as Miss Ford and wore no wedding ring was no indication that she was single. Married women looking for excitement often disguised their marital status and didn't wear their wedding bands.

There could be a Mr. Ford in the picture, but he didn't have the courage to ask such a personal question. It was too soon, and he didn't want to give the impression that he was coming on to her. Then again, maybe she was one of those women who booked cruises only to have affairs. A frown hardened his chiseled features as he tossed his head back and downed the remainder of his drink.

He knew it was natural to have doubts about Melanie, especially after all he had seen on his cruises. And what other reason would a woman have for traveling on a ship alone than seeking a man's companionship? It was the obvious explanation for her trip, but why was it bothering him more than he cared to admit? She was, after all, someone he had only just met. The cruise was short, and he probably would never see her again. So why did it matter to him that she might be looking for a fling?

Well, he was going to put the little schoolteacher out of his thoughts. If she was looking for someone to have an affair with, that was none of his business. He had his job to do, and the less he saw of her, the better off he would be.

With this matter resolved, a yawn sneaked up on him. A good sign, he thought. At least, he'd be able to get a good night's sleep. Tomorrow, he would get up early and do some laps in the pool. That should burn off some of his excess energy. And if that didn't help, he'd put his jogging shoes on and run around the ship. It might knock him out, but it would do the trick.

He yawned again. Placing his empty glass on the desk next to him, he prepared to get ready for bed.

CHAPTER TWO

Standing, dressed in her blue bathing suit, Mel ventured a look at her face in the mirror. To her dismay, she saw what she had expected—dark circles underscored her eyes! Her night of tossing and turning had left its telltale sign. In fact, her overall appearance was lackluster, and she hoped that an early-morning swim might refresh her.

She quickly pulled on her terry-cloth robe, grabbed her sunglasses, and headed for the door. As she walked toward the swimming pool, she felt as if she had to pull every bone in her body. She shook her head. She was here for rest and relaxation, and she felt she'd been run over by a Mack truck. Something was terribly wrong, she moaned to herself. And if she didn't feel better soon, she had the feeling that this would set the stage for the rest of the cruise.

Eagerly approaching the Olympic-sized pool, she took off her robe and sunglasses. Timidly sticking her toe into the pool, she found the water was cooler than she liked. Taking a deep breath and bracing herself, she slowly lowered her body into the water, then pushed off and swam. After finishing a couple of laps, Mel did feel better. The water had revived her, and she no longer minded its temperature. Turning onto her back, she floated, as peacefulness enveloped her. She closed her eyes.

Moments passed before something disturbed her tranquillity. Curious, she opened her eyes. To her surprise, she saw Jim at the other end of the pool, standing on the diving board. There was no denying he had a well-tanned and beautiful body. And she couldn't deny how sexually aroused she was as a wave of excitement rippled through her. His body arched as Jim performed a graceful swan dive before plunging into the water.

Immediately Mel turned onto her stomach and swam toward the side of the pool. For the first time in her life, she wished that she were a faster swimmer. It wasn't that she was running away from him; it was just that she didn't trust herself. He was too attractive to be around. She had to distance herself from this man so she could get her feelings into perspective.

Her slim body glided through the water effortlessly. Just as she saw the rim of the pool and thought she was home free, she felt a body alongside of her. As she reached for the bar to pull herself out of the pool, Jim's head suddenly popped up next to her.

"Hi!" Water dripped off his forehead and lashes, and a grin was plastered across his face.

He was so close that her breath was taken away. She breathed in, but no air reached her lungs.

"You all right?" he asked with concern.

Finally, her breath came in short, quick gasps. "Yes, thank you. I guess I got a little winded," she managed.

"You looked so content floating. I hope I didn't disturb you," he said regretfully.

36

"No, not at all, I was ready to get out," she said a little nervously.

He stared at her as if he were weighing her words, making her feel extremely self-conscious. Her hair was matted against her head, and she was certain that what little mascara she had on was smudged under her eyes. She wanted to ask him what he was thinking, but was afraid to.

"I'm glad I ran into you," he suddenly said in a very friendly way.

"You are?" she asked in a lilting voice.

"Yes, I wanted to tell you how much I enjoyed your company last night," he said cheerfully.

"Thank you."

"It's not that often I meet such a lovely, intelligent woman," he stated appreciatively.

"Thank you," she said again, feeling more foolish by the minute.

He had a way of affecting her that simply sent her pulse racing, throwing her for a loop. Here he was the captain. Why on earth was he coming on to her? Did he think her an easy mark because she was a school-teacher from a small town? With that thought, she frowned.

"What's the matter?" he asked, touching her shoulder.

That did it! If she thought she was on the edge before, the mere touch of his hand sent her reeling. She blushed and then shivered, and she knew she had to put distance between them. She looked at him hopelessly. An amused glint came into his baby-blue eyes, and Mel had the distinct feeling that he was aware of her frustration and could take advantage of it.

"I'm getting cold," she quickly stated, and without a further word, turned.

"See you later," he called after her.

She swung back to face him. He was smiling, a bright, heartwarming look. She automatically offered a small smile in return.

" 'Bye," she said softly, and then continued along her way.

As she walked almost the length of the pool, water sluicing off her body, she could feel his eyes on her. She quickened her stride as she headed for her robe. With great dignity, she slipped it on, put on her sunglasses, and casually strolled away.

Once out of view, she took off, hurrying to her room. Opening the door, she slammed it behind her. Still shaking from the encounter with the Viking, she reached for a glass of wine to steady her nerves. Slowly sipping the dry liquid, she felt better. But then she was instantly annoyed—annoyed at herself for being so vulnerable, running away like a scared rabbit. She had to get hold of herself, she warned, or she would lose all self-respect. It was inconceivable that one mere man should have so much control over her. Was she a woman or a schoolgirl with her first crush?

She set her drink down sharply. The thought of her acting so foolishly disturbed her even more. She was determined not to let some Casanova captain work his charms on her. No, she wouldn't allow that to happen. No matter how attracted to the guy she was, she would resist him at all costs.

She suddenly thought that perhaps she should work on the article, but she wasn't in the mood. Her wet suit felt like a clammy straitjacket, and she had to take it off. Slipping out of her clothes, she decided to take a shower. As the water poured over her body, it felt refreshing and aroused her. The man was already in her blood. Just the thought of him made her nipples grow taut. And she suddenly wondered if it was really so bad to feel excited. She had never felt so alive in her life. But he was not good for her. What a dilemma! She suddenly wondered whether some other woman had stood in the same, exact shower, thinking about the captain and wondering what to do. This thought upset her and she abruptly turned off the water and stepped out of the stall.

Briskly drying herself, she reminded herself that he was only a man, flesh and bones, and she could handle him.

All of a sudden she was hungry and decided to have some lunch. Then perhaps to keep herself busy, she would take in some shuffleboard and deck tennis.

Satisfied with her plan of action, her spirits were lifted, and she proceeded to get dressed.

The captain began his routine rounds with his staff, checking the tide schedule at various ports of call, examining the fuel gauge and setting the ship's knot speed. He also inquired of the ship's doctor whether any illnesses had affected the passengers. Then he went below to ask the purser how the travelers seemed to be enjoying the voyage. Confident that all was in order, he strolled across the deck and looked out over the ocean. How many of these trips had he taken? Too many to count. He had never expected that he would ever think that. But the offer of a ship-safety business partnership with a close friend appealed more to him every day.

The waves roared and crashed into the side of the ship as a cool breeze ruffled his hair. Discontent threatened his tranquillity. Jim could no longer deny his desire to settle down and have a family. But it wasn't until this very moment that he had become acutely aware of this. Maybe it was because he had finally met someone that he wanted to share his life with. He knew that it sounded corny, but it was the truth. It was not until he had set eyes upon Melanie that he knew his search was over. He would have preferred to meet her under different circumstances. Considering his position, it was difficult for him to approach her, as he didn't want to give her the impression that he made a habit of coming on to beautiful women, and he had been much bolder in the swimming pool than he had intended. But when he saw her lovely body, her full bosom accentuated by the low cut of her bathing suit, he couldn't help himself. And he knew that she had been somewhat taken with him. His experience had taught him that much about women.

He sighed. He knew that he had to proceed with caution. They didn't know each other very well, and a misunderstanding could easily occur. He didn't know what her modus operandi was. She seemed somewhat naïve, but just because she blushed easily didn't mean that she was. She could be just as deceptive and out for a fling as the next woman.

And she knew nothing about him. How could she possibly know that the kind of feeling he felt for her was a first for him? No, she had no way of knowing that, nor did he have any indication that it would even matter if she did. He knew that she had found him sexually attractive, but that had nothing to do with the kind of caring he was talking about.

But he still wasn't comfortable with his reaction to her. It was too quick, too strong, and he doubted its permanence. Infatuation was simply not the same as love. He needed to spend time with her, more time than the cruise allotted, to prove the validity of his feelings.

He glanced at his watch. It was time to dress for dinner. He looked forward to seeing her again, seeing her lovely eyes and beautiful smile. He suddenly wondered how a grown man could so easily be reduced to putty in a woman's hand. A smile curled up the corners of his mouth. It wasn't such a bad thought if the hand happened to belong to Melanie.

Abruptly he turned and strolled with an air of purpose toward his cabin.

Mel woke with a start. Something had pulled her out of her sleep, but she didn't have the foggiest idea what it was. Then an alarm went off in her head. What time was it? Oh, no, she thought as she glanced over at her travel alarm. It took her bleary eyes a few minutes to focus, and she hoped that she hadn't slept through dinner. Seven. She still had time to make it. Jumping out of bed, she made a dash for the bathroom. Halfway into the room, it dawned upon her that tonight was Fancy Dress Night and she was supposed to wear a costume. She sighed deeply and turned on the faucets. While she waited for the water to get warm, she rifled through her clothes trying to decide what she

41

could wear. She critically eyed the room. Her glance fell on the bed. Not very original, but it might do, she thought with renewed optimism. She immediately turned on her heel and headed for the shower.

Mel took small steps as she walked down the corridor toward the dining room. Feeling a little ridiculous with a sheet wrapped around her, she wondered whether anyone might get the idea that she was supposed to be a Roman senator's wife. She also hoped that her rhinestone pins would keep the cloth securely in place.

It seemed as if it took her forever to reach her destination. As she entered the dimly lit large room, a multitude of colorful costumes and merriment assailed her. Mel smiled as she watched the festive group. The officers all looked crisp in their white duck trousers, white buckskin shoes, and open-throated white shirts with short sleeves. On their shoulders they wore their insigne of rank. To her amazement, she found quite a few sheet-wrapped men and women, looking more like spooks than anything else. So, after all, she wasn't the only one who had forgotten to pack or rent an appropriate outfit for this special occasion.

Feeling more at home, she moved to the center of the room and took an offered glass of wine. As she stood, slowly sipping her drink, a pregnant lady and a clown approached, waving enthusiastically at her. Her first instinct was that they knew her, but she didn't recognize them. Then an awful thought came to mind. Perhaps her disguise had become unraveled? With a gasp, she glanced down at her sheet. The quick, sharp movement almost caused her to spill her drink. Relieved that the layers of her costume were still intact, she stared back at the smiling couple, baffled.

"My, don't you look cute, but scary!" the clown announced cheerfully.

Mel laughed. She would recognize that bubbly voice anywhere. "Peg, I didn't know that was you!" Mel exclaimed happily. "But this is supposed to be a Roman toga, not a shroud for a ghost," she explained with amusement.

"You could have fooled me," Peg piped with laughter.

Then Mel noted that the pregnant lady was frowning at her and asked, "But who . . ."

"Is it the stomach that throws you off?" Peg immediately interrupted with a chuckle.

Then the pregnant lady let out a deep, throaty roar, and Mel broke into a round of laughter.

Finally when she was able to speak, she declared, "Joe, you're too much! Where'd you get that blond wig?"

"It's a good one, isn't it?" Peg stated, slapping her side as she laughed.

Joe chuckled and retorted, "It's really Peg's. She uses it when she goes out on the town without me!"

Peg playfully shot him a dirty look and retaliated with, "And here all the time I thought you were sleeping!"

Mel laughed. It was good to be with this friendly couple, and she felt it was a good omen that she had started off the evening in their company.

"Did you see all that food?" Peg asked enthusiastically, her blue eyes getting bigger.

"No, I just got here," Mel answered.

"Peg wants one of each," Joe teased his wife.

"I think I do, too. I'm starving," Mel exclaimed, feeling very relaxed and happy.

"Well, let's get in line," Peg suggested, and they turned in the direction of the long white buffet covered with the grand feast.

Mel felt as content as a fat cat as she sipped her coffee and stared out at the couples dancing on the dance floor. The food had been excellent, Peg and Joe were wonderful company, and she was really starting to enjoy herself. She had noted some of the single women passengers being paired off with officers, but luckily no one had approached her. Not even the good-looking captain. She had caught him looking in her direction on more than one occasion, but he had not given her any sign of recognition. She wondered what had put a kibosh on his naturally aggressive behavior. Perhaps the happily married older couple with her had struck a chord in his guilty conscience.

Watching the couples made her acutely aware how alone she was. Being by herself had never bothered her before, but after seeing Jim, it was difficult for her to sit there and not want to be in his arms.

As if on cue, someone took her arm, and Mel instinctively thought it was Jim.

She turned quickly with a broad smile written across her face. To her mortification, it was the young officer with the hungry eyes peering down at her.

"Happy to see me?" he asked, tickled pink.

"Oh, hello," she replied stiffly.

"You're Miss Ford, right?"

"Yes."

He smiled. "My name is Tom West." He ran his hand lightly up her arm, which she stubbornly stared at before shaking it free.

"If I didn't know better, I would have thought you were avoiding me," he said, leaning closer to her.

Moving backward, she inquired, "What makes you say that?"

"I've been looking for you, I hope you haven't found somebody else," he said brazenly.

"If you don't mind . . ."

"How about a dance?" he asked eagerly.

"Well . . ."

"Come on, the song has just begun," he said quickly, and she was up and onto the dance floor before she even knew what had happened.

He held her a little tighter than she liked, and she found herself inching away every chance she got.

"Loosen up," he whispered, his mouth hot against her ear, and Mel automatically retaliated by stepping on his foot.

"Oh, I *am* sorry," she said demurely.

"Well, don't let it happen again," he retorted, and then laughed as though he'd just told the funniest joke.

"Can't promise," she answered lightly.

The young officer suddenly stared down at her intensely. "I hope the Miss indicates that you're single. Not that I haven't been with married women," he boasted, and then went on, "but unattached women turn me on more."

Mel smiled sweetly and replied, "You may draw your own conclusion."

An awkward smile crossed his face, and his body

stiffened a little, but they were the only indications that he even heard her words.

Luckily the song was over, and Mel started to walk away, but, because of her sheet, she could only take tiny steps. Another song started and Tom had her in his clutches again. She half heartedly swayed to the beat and wondered how on earth she could extricate herself from this man.

Suddenly the words "Excuse me," followed by a tap on Tom's shoulder, instantly made the couple stop dead in their tracks.

Somewhat relieved, Mel saw Jim's smiling face.

"May I cut in, Mr. West," he declared, peering down at the younger officer.

"Oh, certainly, sir," the young officer responded immediately.

And Mel got the feeling that the man was shaking in his boots and she had to stifle a grin.

Tom nodded and walked away. Her hazel eyes trailed after him, making certain that he was definitely a safe distance away.

"Would you like to dance?" Jim asked, pulling her around to face him.

"Yes, thank you," she said politely, looking up into his devilish blue eyes.

He smiled his sunny smile, and took her into his arms, pulling her close to him. She could feel the strength of his arms, the hardness of his chest, and the smoothness of his skin as her head rested against his chin. Her body never felt so alive, and she wondered if she was dreaming. All of her defenses melted away, and she knew how easy it would be to fall victim to this man's charm. She smiled to herself. She was glad that he had rescued her from Tom, but she wasn't certain which of the two was worse. With the young officer, she had felt put upon, but with Jim, she felt as if her whole being were in jeopardy. But she was determined not to become another one of his conquests, and she promised herself to do her best to resist him.

The music miraculously ended, and she was able to separate herself from him.

"How about a cordial?" he asked warmly.

"Fine," she answered.

He took her arm, and they headed toward the bar. But his stride was too quick, and she said, "You'll have to slow down a bit. I'm getting caught up in my sheet."

He laughed. "Sorry about that. I meant to tell you what a cute mummy you make."

Mel glared at him, wondering what he was implying.

"That's what you're supposed to be, isn't it? A mummy?"

Then it dawned upon her—an Egyptian mummy! "Oh, no!" she exclaimed with a laugh. "I'm supposed to be a Roman senator's wife and this is my toga," she explained, touching her cloth.

"Oh, and here I thought all those other people were mummies," he declared with a chuckle.

"Yes, I've noticed how original my outfit is," she returned with a touch of irony in her voice.

"You're right, you wouldn't win the contest for originality, but you *are* the cutest old bones around."

Mel couldn't help laughing. "You definitely have a way with words," she exclaimed.

"I know," he said, seemingly very proud of himself.

47

"How about that drink?" she asked, and he nodded.

They took a table, and as a steward approached, they both ordered a Courvoisier. Sipping and inhaling the warm, smooth brandy, Mel couldn't believe how calm she was with Jim.

"I feel relaxed with you," Jim said, almost echoing her thoughts.

"Thank you," she said simply.

"I hope you don't think I'm giving you a line."

Mel stared into his blue eyes and noted the seriousness etched there. What could she tell him without offending him? She smiled weakly. "What made you say that?"

He glanced down at his brandy snifter. Then raising his eyes back to her, he said, "It's just that I know how you might think that. Don't get me wrong, it has nothing to do with me. I mean personally. But when people are on a ship, everything seems more romantic. At least, many of the passengers think so."

Was this man trying to tell her not to make more of his words than was intended? "Don't worry, I wouldn't dream of letting the moonlight dazzle my judgment," she retorted.

"Of course not, Melanie," he said with a hint of sadness in his voice. "Since I'm the captain of this ship and meet a lot of women passengers, people might think that I spend a lot of time with them. But it's not so," he went on.

"You don't owe me any explanations."

"That's where you're wrong. I want to get to know you, and I want to make sure that you understand my position."

"I'm flattered that you feel that way, but the cruise

will be over soon, and we may never see each other again," she stated, wondering just what he was up to.

"Well, it doesn't have to be that way," he offered with bright eyes.

Mel immediately took a sip of her drink. She was afraid to reach for the carrot he was dangling. "I'm beginning to hope this trip will never end," she exclaimed, changing the subject.

Her avoidance of his words didn't escape him, but he didn't mention it. "I'm glad you feel that way."

"Well, I must admit, I did have a lot of reservations about making this cruise alone."

"You aren't married, right?" he asked.

Darn! She had left herself open for that question, and it was the second time this evening that it had been asked. "No, I'm not. And what about you?" she ventured.

"No, of course not," he immediately replied.

By his tone, he sounded a bit edgy. She stared at him with a quizzical look.

"You've just proved my concern is valid," he explained.

"I don't understand."

"If I were married, Melanie, I wouldn't be sitting here with you right now."

Mel blushed. He had driven his point home, and she suddenly felt very stupid. But that didn't mean that his womanizing should be overlooked.

"Well, there are quite a few married men who do fool around. Not that I meant you would," she quickly responded.

"That's true, but I would never be one of them. Marriage is too sacred to me. It means sharing my life

with someone for better or worse, and it means forever."

"That's a very nice way to think of it," Mel interjected.

"That's the only way to think of it," he corrected harshly.

She could tell he was a man who didn't like to be argued with, and she knew when to leave well enough alone. "The subject is closed," she declared with a laugh.

"I didn't mean to be so overbearing about it. It's just that I feel very strongly about making a commitment to someone," he stated.

"Then why are you still single?" she asked quickly.

The minute the words were out of her mouth, she regretted them. By asking such a personal question, she was practically telling the man how attractive she found him.

"Why did you ask that?" he inquired, his blue eyes intense.

"Well, I'm certain you don't have any problems meeting women," she answered casually, hoping she'd covered her tracks.

"Sure, I meet plenty of women, but I am a very choosy man. Not all women appeal to me."

"I see," she said.

"No, I don't think you do," he said, cocksure of himself.

He was deliberately baiting her, but she was determined not to give him any more encouragement. "Your social life is your business, not mine," she retorted, took a sip of brandy, and nonchalantly looked out at the dance floor.

"So why are you so upset?"

The moment of truth had come to her, but his question had suddenly taken her unaware. "What makes you think that?" she inquired, hedging.

"Just a feeling," he replied.

Mel stubbornly refused to answer his question and kept her eyes glued in the direction of the dance floor.

"Care to dance again?" he asked.

Normally she would have accepted his offer. Dancing would definitely have been a way to change the subject. But being in his arms twice in one night was too much of a temptation to handle.

Turning back to him, she said, "No, thank you. I was just watching Peg and Joe Harper. They seem so happy."

"Oh, yes, the older couple. Joe's dressed as the pregnant woman, and she's the clown?"

"Yes, that's them."

"I didn't know they were your friends," he said, surprised.

"I just met them on the cruise," she explained.

"I still don't understand why a beautiful woman such as yourself would choose to travel alone," he said with keen interest.

She looked at him. Was he fishing to find out if she had a boyfriend, or that she was looking for a fling?

"I don't mean to be rude, but why does that interest you?" she asked point-blank.

"I want to know about you, I want to know everything about you," he declared emphatically.

The emotion in his voice suddenly made Mel feel that maybe he was telling her the truth. But she was too attracted to him and felt too vulnerable in his presence to trust her own instincts. She had too much at stake to take him seriously.

"I don't know what to say," she finally voiced.

He sipped his drink and then looked down into his glass as he shook the liquid. He suddenly seemed disturbed about something, and Mel wondered if he had regretted his show of emotion, especially since she hadn't responded very well to him.

"You seem cautious, as if you don't trust me," he said abruptly.

"I really don't know you," she came back.

"That's true, but I hope you'll give me the time to get to know you," he stated.

"We're getting to know each other, aren't we?" she asked evasively.

He smiled, as if he knew what she was up to. "Sure," he said, and shrugged.

She could tell he was getting discouraged, and she couldn't blame him. But she really couldn't tell him what she suspected about him—that he took advantage of lonely women passengers. No, she couldn't tell him that.

They were silent as they stared out at the dancing couples and sipped their brandy.

Finally, the silence between them became awkward, and Mel decided that it was best that she retire for the evening. "Well, I think I'd better get some sleep. I'm a little tired."

"Fine," he said, rising as she stood up.

"Thank you for an enjoyable evening," she said, offering him her hand.

But he made no attempt to take it. "I'll walk you back to your cabin."

"No, that's all right," she insisted.

"I'm not going to bite. I am the captain of this ship, and I do have a reputation to maintain. So you don't have to worry that I'll do anything out of line. I only want to make sure that you are safe and sound."

His blue eyes had turned cold, and she knew that she had pushed the wrong button, and had been politely told off.

"Thank you," she said, without further objection, and turned to leave.

Jim walked alongside her as they slowly made their way to her cabin. Once they reached her door, he waited as she took her key out of her purse and unlocked her door.

As the door opened, he murmured, "Good night."

"Good night," she answered.

He stared at her, studied her, as if he wanted to read her thoughts. It seemed as though he wanted to ask her something, but changed his mind. He then turned abruptly and strolled away.

After entering her cabin, she proceeded to get ready for bed. But as soon as her head hit the pillow, she was wide awake. She had visions of a red-headed Viking hovering in her room. She couldn't get James O'Dowd out of her thoughts. And the question that gnawed at her the most was whether she could possibly be wrong about him. Since his behavior toward her had been polite and thoughtful, how could she still believe that he was trying to make the scene with her? She was beginning to believe that he was truly interested in getting to know her. If only that were true, she would surely be in heaven!

She turned onto her side, raised her knees and

curled into a ball. Perhaps she had been too much on guard with him. He had tried to talk to her tonight, and she hadn't given him any encouragement. She had allowed what she had heard about officers putting the make on women passengers to influence her too much. Maybe now was the time to open up with Jim and give him a chance. Besides, she decided, if she were to do justice to the article, she had to be more objective. A Cheshire grin spread across her face. Good point, she thought, glad that she had justified her desire to be with him. Suddenly a calmness came over her, and she closed her eyes. She couldn't wait for tomorrow to come. It was going to be a great day!

A full moon cast its golden streak across the black waves. Jim, shoving his hands into his pockets, wished at a time like this that he still smoked. Being with a woman like Melanie and not being able to touch her was enough to drive any man crazy. He wanted her more than he had ever wanted a woman in his life, and he didn't know why it wasn't working out. Why had she remained so aloof? He had made it quite apparent that he was attracted to her and wanted to get to know her. But she hadn't seemed very impressed. That was a new one for him. He hadn't met a woman yet that hadn't been impressed by him. He knew that sounded conceited, but it was the truth. For some reason, women on the cruise had found his captain's uniform and perhaps what was in it very appealing too. But not her. She was doing almost everything to turn him off. Maybe that was part of the attraction: the challenge of the pursuit. He hoped not, but it was possible. But whatever it was, her mystique, her mystery, it didn't matter. He wanted to know her, inside and out, and he was a very determined man.

He turned and rested his back against the railing, staring across the deck. He never thought he'd see the day when he was ready to disregard his principle of not pursuing the women passengers. He had seen other officers make a work of art of seducing them, and he also knew that some of these women had actually booked the cruise only to experience an exciting fling with one of the officers. So, he could never really blame the officers for their behavior. But sometimes he did feel that they took advantage, and this bothered him. And he really didn't think she was looking for a fling, but he still wasn't sure. He hoped that in the next few days he would be able to find out what made Miss Melanie Ford tick.

CHAPTER THREE

Mel was up at the crack of dawn, feeling rested and looking forward to seeing Charlotte Amalie, St. Thomas, U.S. Virgin Islands. Choosing her favorite blue spaghetti-strapped dress and wide-brimmed, straw hat, she hurried to have a cup of coffee and some fruit before the ship anchored.

The hot sun beat down on her fair skin as she sat in a deck chair, facing the ocean. She sipped steaming coffee while she reflected upon the events of her last few days. Her doubts about taking the cruise had subsided. Her decision to be more open-minded about the captain had made an incredible difference.

His gorgeous eyes and sunny smile came to mind. Wondering where he was, she turned to scan the people on the deck. A tall redhead like Jim was easy to spot, but he was nowhere in sight. What could he possibly think of her after last night? She had been pretty rough on him, but hoped her behavior hadn't discouraged him too much. That would be the irony of it. Just when she had decided that she had unfairly judged him and would now try to be more objective, he might no longer be interested in her. That was a good possibility. But then again, if that's all it took to dampen his ardor for her, it was better to know that now rather than later.

Suddenly a white cap appeared above a group of passengers. There was a tingling in the pit of her stomach as she waited to see if she'd been right. And there he was, bigger than life, and walking directly toward her. *Speak of the devil,* she mused as she smiled to herself. His large frame filled her world. A pleasant, magnetic grin flashed across his face, sending her pulse racing.

He stopped in front of her and peered down, a slight blush coloring his cheeks. Was it possible that he was as happy to see her as she was to see him? A warm tingling sensation overcame her, and she wished that he would move. He disturbed her equilibrium, and she was beginning to feel too vulnerable, too uncomfortable.

"Hello," she said casually, peeking up at him from under her hat.

"I've been looking for you," he declared keenly, not put off in the least by the lack of enthusiasm in her greeting.

"You have?" she asked, more curious.

"Yes, I have," he answered in his rich, deep voice.

A small smile graced her lips as she stared at him. His compelling eyes held her. Trying to break their hold, she glanced down at her cup and wrapped her slender hand around it.

"I was hoping I could buy you dinner tonight," he announced suddenly.

His offer surprised her, and she raised her head. "That sounds great," she answered immediately. Her neck was straining from looking up at him, so she asked, "Would you like to sit down?"

"No, thanks. I have some things to check before we anchor. Then I'll be tied up for a while with the customs people and inspectors from the local islands. What do you say I meet you at Blackbeard's Castle? It's easy to find, just ask one of the local people."

"Blackbeard's Castle," she repeated.

"Yes, you can't miss it."

"Sounds delightful," she exclaimed with a laugh.

"Good. What if I meet you at five in the cocktail lounge at the castle?"

"That's fine," she answered, smiling.

"See you then," he said as she nodded.

He started to leave. Pausing, he took a frank and admiring look at her, his glance dropping from her face to her dress.

She stole a glimpse at his face. His mellow eyes glimmered with the light of desire as a grin softened his serious expression.

"You look great in blue," he remarked appreciatively. "That dress is very becoming to you."

"Better than the sheet?" she asked flippantly, trying to cover her sudden self-consciousness.

"Much better," he retorted with a laugh, then glanced at his watch. "I'd better get going; see you later."

She nodded in agreement as he turned and walked away from her. She watched him as he confidently greeted passengers, his lithe body moving quickly with long, purposeful strides. Her eyes trailed him until he disappeared into the crowd that was waiting for the several launches to take them into the harbor.

She was delighted that everything seemed to be working out perfectly. She had seen her captain, he had appeared to be still enamored of her, and she would be spending time with him on the island. What more could a woman want?

Then as suddenly as her elation had appeared, it also disappeared. It was too good to be true. There had to be a snag somewhere. He was just too damned attractive to be unattached. Women on his previous cruises must have found him as attractive as she had. No woman in her right mind wouldn't jump for the chance to be alone with him. It was a wonder someone hadn't locked her up by now, she thought, remembering how cool she had been to him. But the bottom line was, he *had* gotten her to agree to dinner. Perhaps this gentlemanly act was part of his routine. And just maybe he was a slicker operator than she had given him credit for.

Mel sighed deeply. She wished that she could quiet her mental dialogue. She didn't have the energy to figure any of it out, and she just wanted to push her doubts out of her mind. Tonight she would be with him, and she wanted to have fun. That was the important thing here, and that's what she would concentrate on.

Peg and Joe Harper caught her eye as they waved to her to join them. She smiled, thankful for the distraction, drank the remainder of her coffee, and hurried over to the couple.

They stood at the railing of the ship, watching St. Thomas come into view. The gentle rocking back and forth motion of the sea against the vessel's frame did nothing to dispel her excitement in seeing land again.

The strong breeze played havoc with her hat and she held it tightly as she eagerly awaited the trip to the mainland.

Finally the ship was anchored, and the passengers were transferred to the smaller boats. Once they reached the shore, Peg and Joe asked Mel to accompany them sightseeing. It was obvious that they didn't want her to be alone, and she was very touched by their concern. She thanked the couple, but reassured them that they didn't have to worry about her. She wanted to do some shopping, might join one of the tours, and had plans later for dinner. Her words seemed to satisfy them as they said their farewells and scurried off to see Fort Christian, one of the oldest buildings in America, dating back to 1671.

She smiled at the departing couple. A light breeze blew the wisps of hair which had escaped from under her straw hat across her face. She took in the lovely harbor, the Old World town of Charlotte Amalie, situated at the foot of emerald hills. Tropical birds, lush green foliage, brilliant hibiscus, all shades of bougainvillea, and orchids both wild and cultivated surrounded her. The sight was more beautiful than she had imagined. It was a true island paradise. She glanced up at the sky. It was the most splendid blue, and not a cloud anywhere. The only thing that was missing was someone to share it with, she thought wistfully. And then she thought of her dinner date with Jim and realized that all was not lost yet.

With that happy thought in mind, she decided to join a group of women who were going to craft studios to watch local artisans at work screen-printing fabrics, batiking, tie-dyeing, and dressmaking. From there they would go to see Coral World, a marine complex with a unique underwater tower which went fifteen feet under the surface and had huge windows to view coral reef and exotic marine life. And, if they had time, they would travel to the Adventure Dome to catch the multimedia presentation which transported visitors through the exciting carnival, to explore life under the sea, and to learn about the island people.

Later that day, Mel sat exhausted in an outdoor café, her feet aching, across from two other women with whom she had made friends, sipping a daiquiri. She felt that she had seen enough of Charlotte Amalie, named for the queen of Denmark and capital of the Virgin Islands, to fill a few pages of her article. It was great atmosphere, and she couldn't wait to turn on her tape recorder.

She glanced over at her fellow passengers. Rita, the brunette, was taller and prettier than the blond Lynne. Mel guessed that both of the women were in their late twenties or early thirties, and both were extremely outgoing.

"Have you met any officers yet?" Rita suddenly asked Mel.

Mel looked at the woman and smiled. "Who hasn't?" she declared with a laugh.

"That's what it's all about," added Lynne.

Mel realized that she had been misunderstood, and started to explain, "But that's not . . ."

"But that's not what's here," Rita interrupted, glancing around the tables. "I agree. I can't wait to get back on that ship to get my hands on one of those hunks," she exclaimed with a hearty laugh.

"I'll toast to that," Lynne stated as she raised her glass in salute and tapped Rita's glass.

Mel was relieved that in their excitement the women failed to notice that she hadn't joined in their toast. It was as if someone had just pricked her balloon. Here sat two women who had freely admitted that they were after flings with the officers on the cruise, and who had just shot holes in her theory about how the women were the innocent victims of the good-looking officers. She had just been given some food for thought, and it turned her head around. Never mind what it did to her article.

"How about having dinner with us later?" Rita suddenly asked, jerking Mel out of her thoughts.

She glanced over at Rita and Lynne, who were now standing. "Thanks, but I've already made plans."

"I guess *you* got lucky!" Lynne exclaimed with a slight quiver in her voice.

"Oh, I don't know," Mel quickly said, for lack of anything better.

"Boy, you're modest," Rita declared with a chuckle. Grabbing her purse off the table and swinging it over her shoulder, she said, "Lynne and I are going to scout some of the hotels' cocktail lounges to see if there's anyone interesting. Want to come?"

"No, I think I'll pass. I'm going to rest a bit and finish my drink," Mel answered.

With that the women said their farewells and promptly took off. Mel waited until they were out of sight before taking her tape recorder out of her purse. It was about time she took down some notes, especially her conversation with Lynne and Rita. To be objective, it was important that she include their point of view in her story.

She pressed the record button and talked into the machine. After a few minutes, she suddenly noticed something out of the corner of her eye. Instinctively, she turned to see what it was. To her surprise, she saw Jim walking toward her. Not wanting him to see her tape recorder, she quickly snapped it off and tossed it into her purse.

He was wearing a green shirt and khaki trousers. Even in casual clothes, he looked regal and carried himself with a commanding air of self-confidence. When he waved and smiled, she returned his greeting. She couldn't imagine anyone more exciting to be with on this romantic island.

Within seconds, his long, quick strides had carried him to her table. He stood over her, his hands on his hips. There were touches of amusement around his mouth and near his eyes.

"Fancy meeting you," she said cheerfully.

"It's amazing how fast one can get his work done when he puts his mind to it," he said, his eyes twinkling.

"I'm glad you put your mind to it," she answered happily. "Why don't you take some weight off your feet and sit down?" she teased.

"I thought you'd never ask." He dropped down in the chair opposite her.

He glanced over at her purse, and then back at her. Amusement came into his eyes again. "Are you a spy?"

Damn! Mel thought immediately. The man had

caught her talking into her tape recorder! So that's what he had found so funny when he approached her.

"What made you say that?" she asked nonchalantly.

Jim laughed. "You looked very suspicious the way you talked into that tiny machine of yours!"

Mel shrugged, trying to minimize the importance of his discovery. "I was merely making a record of my trip," she explained coyly.

He cocked an eyebrow. "I'd love to get my hands on that tape recorder."

Mel laughed, a little too nervously—even for her. "I assure you, you would be bored to tears," she said lightly, and sipped her drink.

"Why don't you let me be the judge of that," he retorted with challenging eyes.

Mel looked at him stubbornly. There wasn't any way for him to know what was on the tape, so why was she getting so uptight about it?

"Trust me, you would," she declared flatly, and gazed out at the people passing by.

"Was the trip to the island smooth enough for you?" he suddenly asked, pulling her attention back to him.

"Perfect, hardly felt a thing," she murmured, pleased that they were onto another subject.

"What would you like to do?" he asked.

Suddenly feeling very rejuvenated and happy, she declared, "Whatever you like."

"You're easy," he quipped.

Her eyes narrowed. *How did he mean that?* she wondered.

"That was supposed to be a joke," he said loudly, breaking into her thoughts.

"I hope so," she stated.

"I meant that you're easy about what you want to do, but the rest of you is hard as nails."

She glared at him.

He laughed. "Just trying to get your attention," he teased.

"You like egging me on, don't you?" she asked, without amusement.

"I didn't realize you were so sensitive. I'm sorry," he apologized.

Sensitivity had nothing to do with it. It was the word "easy" that had ticked her off. Why on earth had he chosen that word out of all the many that he could have used? she wondered as she sipped her drink.

"I'm okay. I guess it was just a misunderstanding," she stated.

"I don't understand."

He studied her, waiting. His eyes were gentle, understanding.

How could she tell this man what devious thoughts she had had about him? That he sweet-talked women right into his bedroom? And that she was writing about her cruise and he just might be the villain in the article? No, Captain O'Dowd couldn't imagine how a simple word like "easy" could have triggered all those responses.

"It's a little difficult to explain," she finally said. "I hope you don't mind, but let's just forget it. Okay?"

"Sure," he replied casually.

"Let's have a good time," she said.

A satisfied look came into his eyes. "Now you're talking. How about a banana daiquiri and then a long, leisurely walk on the beach?"

"You know how to live," she came back cheerfully.

"I know this great little place where we can have some banana daiquiris. The tables face the ocean and a terrific combo performs at all times."

Mel cracked a smile, but she wondered how many other ladies he had taken there. He suddenly seemed too slick and overconfident, and this bothered her.

"Or we could go to one of the more popular and elegant hotels if you prefer," he suggested, shoving his big hands into his pockets.

She suddenly realized her face must have telegraphed her thoughts. That was one thing she had never learned to do—to disguise her feelings. And this man had an eerie habit of picking up on her thoughts. It was annoying, to say the least!

"The place you mentioned sounds fine," she answered with a dull edge to her voice.

"Your enthusiasm is overwhelming," he declared with a chuckle as his eyes sparkled a challenge.

"I said what I meant. The first place that you mentioned is where I want to go," she insisted.

"Okay, you're in for a treat, Melanie," he exclaimed. "It's right down the road a few blocks."

"But I don't know if a rum daiquiri would mix with a banana one," she declared with a laugh.

"Sure it will," he said with a smile. "Then we'll have dinner at Blackbeard's Castle."

"Oh, good, I thought you'd forgotten about that place."

"Have you heard about it?" he asked with a curious edge to his voice.

"No, but I like the name," she admitted with sparkling eyes.

"What's in a name?" he asked, and stood. Waiting

for her to follow suit, he answered his own question, "Everything."

Sitting in the restaurant at Blackbeard's Castle with a lovely view of the harbor, Mel didn't think there was any other place on earth where she would rather be.

Jim sat across from her, his folded hands resting upon the table. She wanted to reach out and touch them, but she couldn't. It was hard enough just being in the same room with him, let alone touching his skin.

The day with Jim had been perfect. He was his charming, wonderful self and made her laugh in a way she hadn't laughed in a very long while. He had a way of bringing out a vibrancy in her that she didn't even know she was capable of. And he made her feel important. Every time he spoke to her, his eyes had an unbelievable hue to them. She had to believe that he felt something for her. But she kept reminding herself that she would be going home soon and she would never see him again. That was the only thought that kept her from falling for his line and throwing herself into his arms.

A small smile curled up the corners of her lips.

"A penny for your thoughts," he said quietly.

"Sorry," she exclaimed with a little laugh, "I was daydreaming."

"It must be the boring company you're with," he retorted.

"No, that's not what I meant," she declared. "I was just thinking about the great day I had, and it's really a shame that it has to end."

"I'm glad you feel that way," he admitted, lightly

touching her hand. "It was good for me to take this time away from the ship. You'll never know how good it was for me."

His eyes glistened, pleading for companionship. For one fleeting second, Mel saw and felt his loneliness, but she doubted her reaction to him. A good-looking man like Jim just couldn't be lonely, she reasoned.

"The dinner was great," she stated, changing the subject.

"Yes, it was. Happy you got to see Blackbeard's Castle?"

"It made my day!" she answered with a laugh. "He was an infamous womanizer, wasn't he?" she asked, thinking Jim had a lot in common with the pirate.

"Yes, married fourteen times and killed his brides when the nuptial bliss wore off," Jim announced with a wicked glint to his eyes.

"A woman must be careful whom she marries," she retorted, wide-eyed, playing along with his game.

"And why haven't you gotten married? Too cautious?" he inquired, suddenly more serious.

"I'd prefer not to get into that, if you don't mind," she said flatly.

"I haven't gotten married because I hadn't found the right person to share the rest of my life with," he stated.

"And have you found her now?" she asked brazenly. The moment the question was out of her mouth she wondered what had caused her to be so bold.

"Possibly," he answered, hinting at some dark mystery.

His eyes were intense. Did he want her to believe

that he was talking about her? She had heard lines before, but this one took the cake!

Deliberately glancing at her watch, she announced, "I think it's time we got back to the ship."

Jim looked at his watch and nodded in agreement. "I didn't realize it was so late. I guess that's what happens when you're having a good time."

"Yes, that's true," she murmured.

She couldn't deny that she'd never had a better time. But she was determined not to make more of it than was intended. An invitation to dinner did not make for a lifetime of commitment.

His blue eyes met her hazel ones, and she wondered what secret those brilliant eyes held. When he stared at her that way, she had the feeling that he wanted to ask her something. If her intuition was right, she puzzled over what held him back. Could it be possible that he was shy? Ridiculous! she answered as she watched him turn to summon the waiter for the check.

The ride back to the ship was a quick one. Mel barely remembered getting into the launch, so aware was she of the man next to her. Conversation seemed strained, so they both had slipped into their own thoughts. She had always been in control of her emotions, until she met Jim. There was something about him that totally unnerved her and made her feel like a hopeless schoolgirl with a crush. Yes, she knew the symptoms. She had seen too many of her pupils with their heads in the clouds not to recognize someone in love. But did she love Jim? she wondered. Or was it only infatuation? She had to believe that her feelings for this man were genuine. Yet the practical person that she was wouldn't let her believe that she could fall head over heels in love with a total stranger.

But as they neared the ship, she toyed with the idea of inviting him into her cabin. What would be the harm? she asked. She wanted to be with him, regardless of any doubts about his principles. Her attraction to him outweighed any restraint that she might have, and the pull she felt toward him seemed to jam her logical thought process.

Once they reached the ship, Jim asked, "Would you care for a nightcap?"

"After all those daiquiris, I think I'd pass out," she exclaimed. "But thank you," she added as she noted the disappointment in his eyes.

"Well, I guess I'll walk you to your cabin then."

As they walked through the long corridor, somewhere about halfway down, Mel lost the conviction of her heart. Even though every part of her body cried out to experience this man's mystery, she suddenly felt that she had more to lose than gain. She couldn't put her finger on why she felt that way. Whether it was because he appeared to be more worldly and sophisticated than she, or simply that she had never known such strong feelings and they scared her, it didn't matter. Instinctively, she knew she couldn't risk being alone with Jim.

When they reached her door, an awkwardness came over her as she fumbled in her purse for her key.

Finally, finding the key and holding it up, she announced with a laugh, "Here it is!"

But her attempt at levity was cut short. The look in his eyes warned of something, but she didn't have the foggiest notion of what. Before Mel could think any further, he had her in his arms and was kissing her. She thought her knees would surely buckle, she was so taken aback. She found herself reeling as she experienced the most wonderful sensation. Her whole body tingled with such excitement that she thought she would explode with ecstasy. But before she could reach that plateau, his lips released their hold, and she was left gasping for breath.

Finally regaining her composure, she asked, "What did you do that for?"

"I've wanted to do that from the first moment I saw you, but I was afraid that you'd get the wrong impression of me," he said hoarsely. "Do you mind if I come in?" he asked.

His passionate eyes gave little doubt of his intentions.

Would the spider like to come into the fly's compartment? she wondered immediately. At last he had decided to take the bull by the horns.

"What impression was that?" she asked, stubbornly passing over his question.

"Oh, you know, being the captain and all. I didn't want you to think that I made a habit of coming on to my passengers," he explained.

"And you don't?" she inquired. She hadn't meant to be so blunt. The question just tripped off her tongue. By the twitch along his jawline, she knew he hadn't liked her question.

"No, I don't," he returned assertively. "I would like to see you when the cruise is over, Melanie. I've always made it a rule never to get involved with any of the women on my ship, but this is the first time I've ever met anyone who has made me want to break that rule."

Mel stared at him, not knowing what to think. His kiss had totally sent her for a loop, and now he said that he wanted to see her after the cruise was over. Was this his grand stand to win her over, to trust him enough to invite him into her bed? Her emotions were thrown into turmoil, and a protective haze began to take over.

"Melanie, I really would like to see you," he repeated with earnest.

Oh, sure, she thought sarcastically, afraid to hope that it could be true. The man had just kissed her, and he knew what a gob of jelly she had turned into. He sensed her vulnerability and he was in for the kill.

She smiled politely and said, "I don't know."

"Well, why don't you give me your phone number, and I'll call you. That way, you'll have time to think about it," he suggested.

His words made sense, but she found herself resisting him. "I'd prefer not to," she answered.

He looked at her as though he couldn't believe what she had said, and Mel wondered if this was the first time the captain had been turned down.

"I don't understand," he declared.

"I don't give my number out to strangers," she retorted.

She knew it was a lame excuse, but she didn't want to give her number to him and then wait for a phone call that would never come.

"We've already had dinner together. I don't think of you as a stranger, and I didn't think that you thought

72

that of me, either. If there's another man in the picture, please tell me."

"No, I'm not involved with anyone."

"Well, then, go out with me, and we won't be strangers," he said with his charming smile.

"I'm sorry, Jim, but I don't think I'd better," she stated, more firmly.

"And that's it?"

"Yes," she said simply.

He shrugged. "Okay, so I won't call you, but I think we could have had something worthwhile."

Mel stared at him blankly. None of it made sense to her. She wanted to be with him, but was afraid. She felt as if her life were in jeopardy. It was crazy, but that's exactly how she felt. She couldn't bear to be used like a toy by Jim, especially when she could really care for him. She had to stay away from him, that was all there was to it.

"I guess we'll never know," she said with an edge of sadness in her voice. Turning to her door, she added, "Thank you for the lovely evening. Good night."

"Good night," he replied as she faced him.

An indefinable look came into his eyes. "I'll wait until you get in," he said in a solemn tone.

"Thank you," she replied politely, and inserted the key into the lock.

As the door opened, she glanced back at Jim.

He nodded, and she sighed as she watched him walk quickly away.

CHAPTER FOUR

Mel closed the door quietly and leaned up against it. Her body was trembling. He had to be the most exciting man in the world, and she had just shut him out. He probably thought her crazy, and that was understandable. Her body had given him one signal, while she had given him another. The moment she had not asked him in, she questioned her sanity.

Why did he have to kiss her? she moaned. His action was so impetuous that she couldn't even think straight. All that came to mind was that he had finally made his move, and she was put on the defensive.

Mel automatically shook her head. Everything was timing, and his was definitely off, she thought as she walked over to her bed. She had just decided to trust him, and then he went and kissed her. His kiss had aroused her beyond belief, but triggered her self-defense mechanism. No wonder she refused to give him her telephone number. If only he had waited, even a day, she might have been more in control of the situation.

He said that he wanted to see her after the cruise was over. How could that have been possible? He was stringing her along. Since he had asked for her num-

74

ber, it must have been his signal to maneuver her into bed.

Mulling this over, she slipped out of her dress and put on her robe. So, maybe her reaction to Jim had been right on target, she decided. And perhaps she should stop blaming herself for feeling that she hadn't handled the situation with as much savoir faire as she would have liked.

Thinking about it, Mel was finally satisfied that her response was correct. The man was only interested in sex, maybe a little more patient than most. And if she had given in to her desire to be with him, she would have left herself open to be hurt the morning after. Already her feelings for him had gone much deeper than any one-night stand could satisfy.

A calmness came over her, the way it always did when an answer had been found, a problem solved. Yes, she was no longer at odds with herself, but she didn't feel happy thinking the worst of Jim. It was as if a beautiful fantasy had been shattered into a million pieces. She couldn't deny that on some level she really wanted to believe that he did care for her. But she now felt that there was nothing else she could have done except reject him.

Now the best thing for her to do was to forget about her disappointment and try to relax. Knowing that she wasn't ready to sleep, she picked up the mystery she had brought with her. As she sat on her bed she couldn't help but think what a ridiculous situation it was. Here she was in one of the most romantic settings in the world, with one of the most exciting men at her feet, and she was going to bed with a book. Life wasn't fair, she reasoned, and wondered whether she shouldn't write the article about how to make the best of a lonely cruise. Mel frowned, opened the book, and began to read.

Mel spent the following morning lounging in her cabin, sipping coffee, and working on her article, trying to put the captain out of her thoughts. She recorded the previous day's events, but when she came to the part about his kiss, she had to stop. The memory of his touch was still too devastating, and describing it on the tape recorder somehow didn't seem right. Her experience was too intimate, too personal, and she suddenly had misgivings about writing about it. It would be as though she were exposing herself to the world, and there was a limit to how far she would go in the name of art. Her feelings for Jim were hard enough for her to deal with, much less write about. And how would the captain feel about being included in her article? If he knew that he was being used as a study, put under a jar and examined like some insect, he would, no doubt, be quite perturbed. That would be a given, and she wouldn't blame him if he wanted to choke her. But he would never know about the article, because she was sure that he didn't read women's magazines. Thank goodness for little things, she mused.

She sighed deeply, and put away her recorder. Being restless, she could no longer concentrate. A stroll around the ship was needed to burn up her excess energy. With that thought in mind, she swung her slender legs off the bed and headed for the door.

Her stride was quick as she made her way toward the deck. Some sun suddenly seemed to be the answer for her morose mood. Once she reached her destination, she flopped herself down onto a deck chair.

Moments passed as she stared blankly out at the ocean. Tomorrow she would be back in Florida and then home. She could get on with her life: see her friends, write her article, and do some repairs on her house until the fall school term started. And the cruise would be but a memory, and thoughts of her Viking would fade like the streaks of a golden sunset. Strange how quickly the time went by, she thought. She wondered if Jim would ever think about her. Not for a second, she answered instantly. She wondered what it would have been like to be in his arms, but she'd never know, she thought wistfully.

The sun was hot but comforting. There was something about its brilliant rays that always made her feel better. She decided to get up and to do some shopping. There was still the rest of the day, and she would make the best of it. Perhaps she would join the Harpers for dinner, she thought, feeling more optimistic. Peg and Joe always had a good effect upon her, and she would really miss them.

Knowing how much the couple enjoyed the daily horse racing in the ship's lounge, she thought she would see them first to make sure that they would spend their last evening together. As she hurried to find them, she thought she caught a glimpse of Jim before he disappeared into a group of passengers. Her step faltered, but she wasn't sure and waited a few moments before she continued on her way.

It was early evening when Jim and his First Officer entered the dining area. For the ship's last dinner, formal attire was required, and the room reflected this rule. The women were coiffured, beautifully dressed, and adorned with sparkling jewelry, while the men looked very appealing in their white dinner jackets.

Jim's eyes eagerly traveled over the group. It took him a few minutes before he found the woman he was looking for: Melanie. She was standing with her back to him talking to the Harpers.

He studied her, trying to discover what magic it was that she held over him. The suggestion of delectable curves beneath her black dress was certainly an exciting thought. She wore gold heels, but her legs were hidden. He had seen her sunbathing this afternoon in her white T-shirt and shorts, and now he could visualize her well-proportioned and shapely legs, and each calf that had a sinuous curve leading to a trim ankle. She moved her head, and her rich, glowing auburn hair gleamed like strands of lustrous glass. As she talked, she suddenly gestured with her hand. The recollection of her delicate wrists, leading to strong hands with long, sensitive fingers, made his body ache to experience their touch.

Never before had a woman affected him with such a strong sexual pull, but seldom had a woman rebuffed him so. However, he couldn't deny that her indifference made him want her all the more. She suddenly reminded him of the angel hair that his mother always used at Christmas to decorate their tree. As a young boy he was not immune to its alluring qualities, but he learned it had to be handled carefully when he felt its sharp, cutting edge.

She confused him. Her response to his kiss made him believe that she wanted him as much as he wanted her. So why had she closed the door on him? Women! He'd never figure them out. He had never pursued a woman the way he had pursued Melanie, and where did it get him? Taking a lot of cold showers, that's where! And that was no solution, no matter what the Boy Scouts used to say.

He had wanted her to spend her last evening at his table. It was important to him to show her that her rejection had not daunted him in the least. Like water off a duck's back, he reasoned with a smile. Not wanting to put off the inevitable any longer, he strolled directly over to her.

"Good evening," he said when he reached the Harpers and Melanie.

The older couple looked smilingly up into his face and returned his greeting.

"Hello, Miss Ford," he said pointedly, noticing that she hadn't acknowledged his presence.

Her body stiffened, but she smiled politely. "Hello," she replied with distant eyes.

He smiled at her and wondered what it was that made her seem so fragile. "I wanted you all to join me at my table for dinner," he announced.

"Love to," Joe and Peg agreed simultaneously.

Jim nodded his pleasure and turned to Melanie. "And how about you?" he asked, waiting for her answer.

"I'd be very happy to," she said simply.

He smiled again. He wished he knew what secret was behind her eyes that beckoned to him irresistibly.

"Well, I'm glad that's settled," he said, pleased.

"We'll see you in a little while," Peg quickly interjected as she and Joe started to leave.

Mel hesitated, but Peg pulled her husband along and winked at her when she passed.

Jim's keen eyes didn't miss the interplay between the women.

When Peg was out of earshot, he said, "I guess she thought we wanted to be alone."

"I suppose so," she admitted coolly.

"I'm afraid I was out of line last night, and I want to apologize," he stated.

An indefinable light came into her eyes, and her cheeks blushed. Just the mention of his kiss brought an instant reaction, and Jim knew that he had been right about her wanting him. Then why had she held herself back? There must be another man in the picture.

She shifted her weight under his scrutinizing gaze.

"I didn't mean to stare. I don't want to make you uncomfortable," he said gently, trying to reassure her.

"Thank you for your concern, but I'm fine. And thank you for your apology," she said in a barely audible voice.

"A tan becomes you," he said appreciatively.

"Yes, I did get some sun today," she answered.

"Yes, I saw you," he retorted instantly.

Her eyes narrowed. It was as though a protective shell had just covered her. "You did?" she asked, surprised.

"I did, but I didn't want to disturb you. You seemed so lost in thought," he explained.

"I was," she answered. Then, as an afterthought, she added, "I can't believe how fast the time went."

"Did you have a good time?"

"Better than I had expected," she answered without thinking.

"That sounds as though you had some reservations," he declared.

"Well, it was my first cruise . . ." she stated as her voice suddenly trailed off.

"Anxious to get home?"

She stared at him as though she hadn't heard his words, but he knew that she had. He wondered if she knew what he was getting at. He was hoping that she would give him some reaction that she might miss him, some signal that would let him know that she wanted to see him again. But her expression gave him no indication that she even cared. He wished he knew what she was thinking.

It all seemed so preposterous to her. Here they were, making idle conversation. The man simply didn't know what effect he had on her, or he wouldn't be asking her those questions. Of course, she wanted to get home, but it meant that she would never see him again. Everything had its pros and cons, but she couldn't help feeling that it was a shame that they hadn't met under different circumstances. Then perhaps they might have had a chance to get to know each other.

"What about you?" she suddenly asked.

"I don't understand."

"Won't you be happy to return home?"

"You mean get away from my floating hotel?" he asked with a chuckle.

"Precisely."

"It does get boring after a while. There's only so much water you can look at," he explained.

Mel shot the good-looking captain a knowing look.

"You don't believe me," he stated as though he'd just been highly insulted.

"With all this social activity buzzing around," Mel exclaimed, indicating the people surrounding them, "I don't know when you'd have time to be bored."

"Do you think that's the same as having a meaningful relationship?" he asked with an air of challenge in his voice.

His eyes were cold and assessing as he waited for her to state her case. And Mel got the feeling she suddenly had a glimpse of what a small animal saw in the eagle's eye just before he swooped down upon his prey.

"No, of course not," she insisted. "But I wasn't comparing socializing to a commitment," she retorted.

"Would you care for a drink?" he asked, and Mel couldn't believe that he was changing the subject.

"I'll wait for dinner, thanks," she returned sweetly, pleased that she had made him back down.

"Do you think I make a habit of kissing all the women passengers?" he inquired with a devilish glint in his eyes.

So his question about the drink was his way of getting the pleasantries of being a host over with, and now he was zeroing in on what was bothering him.

"I don't know, *do* you?" she asked stubbornly, refusing to let him corner her like some fox on a hunt.

"It's a shame you don't know me better," he declared.

There was an arrogance about him, but to Mel's surprise, she thought she detected regret in his voice.

"Yes, I suppose it is," she agreed.

Then maybe she would be certain, once and for all,

what this man was all about. "Do you spend much time on the ocean?" Mel asked, curious about his profession and wishing to change the subject.

"Three months on, and one month off," he replied.

"You mean you're traveling for three months straight?" she questioned, wondering how on earth he could have a relationship.

"Yes, and you thought I was kidding when I said it gets boring. Sometimes the problems get on your nerves too. You get to a point where you just don't want to hear another problem."

He paused and a grin spread across his face.

"What's so funny?" she asked lightly.

"I'm telling *you* my problems," he declared with a chuckle. "I don't know why that is."

"What?"

"I'm usually a pretty close-mouthed individual, but with you, I seem unable to stop talking about myself," he explained.

She could see that he was suddenly uncomfortable as he fidgeted with his hands and then shoved them into his pockets.

"Are you getting tired? Would you like to sit down?" he asked with concern.

"I'm fine," she exclaimed. "Please go ahead, I'm listening."

"Do you like teaching?"

"Yes, very much."

"Have to have a lot of patience, don't you?"

"Yes, at times," she agreed.

She stared up into his beautiful eyes and wondered: Why all the questions?

"Do you think you'll take another cruise?" he asked.

"No," she replied, shaking her head.

"Well, you certainly know how to deflate a guy's ego," he exclaimed playfully.

"It has nothing to do with the cruise. It was perfect," she explained with a little laugh in her voice. "It's just that this trip will last me for a while," she stated.

A sadness came over her as a sense of loss enveloped her. She had wanted to be with this man, to experience him. Regrets were often hard to live with.

"Melanie, are you all right?" he asked, pulling her out of her thoughts.

"Yes, of course," she lied with a smile. "Excuse me, please. I think I'll go find the Harpers to see if they're ready to be seated."

He glanced at his watch. "It's that time already," he stated in disbelief.

"I'll see you at your table," she said, and started to turn.

"I'll look forward to it," he returned, his words halting her step.

An easy smile played at the corner of his lips. For one split second he reminded her of an innocent child. He was so open and trusting, while she had already begun to distance herself from him. She would be leaving the ship tomorrow and would never see him again. She couldn't bear to stand there any longer and pretend that they had forever to talk to each other.

She offered him a small smile in return and continued on her way. She had just said good-bye, and he didn't even know it.

* * *

It was early morning, the last day of the cruise, and Mel found herself strangely moody. After the night before, she thought that she had resolved her compunction about leaving. It was for the best. Her mental tug of war about Jim would no longer exist and her discomfort would be over.

As she packed, she knew that she should be happy about returning home, but she couldn't help wondering what it would have been like to be in Jim's strong arms, regardless of the consequences. It annoyed her that she couldn't shake her attraction for him.

She had risen early to take a quick swim and have breakfast. But she couldn't forget the way Jim had looked at her across the table. His eyes, glowing with a savage inner fire, seemed to be telling her something—something now she would never know. She had taken the easy way out and made sure that she sat as far away from the captain as possible. Then, after breakfast, she had retired to her cabin, not giving him the opportunity to approach her.

Finished packing, she closed her suitcase and made a quick survey of the room to make certain that she hadn't left anything. Satisfied she hadn't, she picked up her suitcase and started to leave. As she reached the door she turned back to take one last look. The little cabin would be stored in her memory forever.

The ship had docked. Crowds of screaming well-wishers gathered below. Mel walked toward the gangplank. She had said her good-byes to Peg and Joe, and she wondered where Jim was. Staring down at the waiting people, she stalled awhile, hoping to see him.

Finally she gave up. It was getting late, and she did have a plane to catch.

Shrugging, she picked up her suitcase and as she joined the line of passengers streaming off the ship, she suddenly caught sight of a white cap, towering over the group. The same tense feeling grabbed at the pit of her stomach. It had to be him. As she neared the cap, she discovered that she had been right. The good-looking captain was standing in profile, talking to the same attractive blonde whom she had seen him with before. The woman laughed and opened her purse, taking out a small card and pen. Quickly writing something on the card, she handed it to Jim and dropped the pen into her purse. Jim smiled and put the card into his jacket pocket.

A twinge of jealousy swept through Mel as she realized that he had probably used the same telephone number technique on that woman, but this time he had gotten lucky. She had seen enough. Disgusted, she wanted to hurry off the boat, but because of the crowd in front of her, her progress was unfortunately slowed.

Then she heard Jim calling after her, "Melanie, wait a minute!"

She stopped dead in her tracks. She didn't want him to think that she was running off like some scared rabbit. She turned slowly on her heel and found herself glaring up into his bewildered-looking face.

"Yes?" she inquired in a low tone.

"You weren't even going to say good-bye."

Sadness had echoed in his voice. *What an actor!* she thought with irritation. Too bad it wasn't Emmy time.

"You were busy, I didn't want to interrupt you,"

she stated coolly, annoyed with herself for still having feelings for the bounder.

A nerve twitched along his jawline and his eyes darkened. "I hope you have a pleasant trip home," he said in a voice that chilled her to the bone.

"Thank you," she said simply, and to her dismay, felt her eyes water.

Not wanting to give him the satisfaction that she cared, without another word she walked away, intuitively feeling his eyes, like daggers, on her back. Her body stiffened as she hurried down the gangplank.

Jim suddenly knew what the expression being left in the lurch meant. He was totally baffled by her behavior. Why such coldness? What had he done to make her treat him the way she had? Perhaps she wanted to have an affair with him after all, and felt rejected. Ridiculous, he answered. He had let her know that he wanted to be with her, and all she had to do was give him the go-ahead sign. But she hadn't. So, what was her problem? Was she afraid of her sexuality?

He watched her slim form until it disappeared out of view. He couldn't believe how attractive he found her. Not only was she a beautiful woman, but also an intelligent one: a winning combination. If one of his friends had told him a few days ago that he would have fallen for a schoolteacher, he would have told him that he was crazy. And by her reaction to his kiss, she seemed to like him too. A man knew that about a woman, he explained to himself. But why had she not followed her impulse to be with him?

She was a mystery to him, one that he wanted to solve. He knew that he wanted to see her again, even though everything in his whole being warned against it. She was bad news, and he would be smart to stay away from her. But she was also a challenge, and one that he wouldn't back down from. In two weeks he would have a job interview in Pittsburgh, and he was determined to get in touch with her then. Even though the practical side of his character called him masochistic, it didn't matter. For one unguarded moment he'd caught a glimpse into her heart, and he felt that she *did* have feelings for him. He had seen the emotion in her eyes just before she turned and walked out of his life. And it was enough for him to seek her out to find out what the truth of her feelings was. He was enough of a romantic possibly to make a fool of himself for the sake of passion.

The taxi stopped in front of Mel's Georgian house. As she paid the fare, she couldn't believe that she'd been away less than a week. It seemed like ages since she left, but she was glad to be home. Stepping out of the cab, she closed the door behind her and took a deep breath. The return trip had been a long one, and she was suddenly weary and hungry. She glanced over at her yard. It was early evening, but still light enough for her to see that the lawn needed mowing and the shrubbery needed pruning. She certainly had enough to occupy her for the next few days.

Wondering what she could eat, she headed up the steps to her house. When she reached her door and opened her purse to get out her keys, she heard her phone ringing. Opening the door, she set her suitcase down and rushed for the phone.

Jim strangely came to mind, and she wondered if

somehow he had obtained her number. She suddenly wished that he had, as she made a mad dash to pick up the receiver before the phone stopped ringing.

"Hello," she answered, slightly out of breath.

"Hi there, stranger," came Helen's cheerful voice.

"Oh, hi, Helen," she responded with a tinge of disappointment in her voice.

"Did I catch you at a bad time?" her friend asked, obviously catching the tone in her voice.

"No, I just walked in," Mel explained.

"I won't keep you then, but how did it go?"

The eagerness in her friend's voice made Mel laugh. "It's hard to put in words, but I'm glad I went," Mel declared.

"You better be able to put it into words. Excuse the pun," Helen exclaimed with a laugh. "Let's meet for lunch tomorrow, and you can tell me all the torrid details."

Mel laughed again. "It certainly was an eye-opener."

"Worse than we thought," Helen said with awe.

"You'll have to wait till tomorrow to find out," Mel teased.

"How can I sleep?" Helen asked, protesting.

"Like a baby," Mel came back playfully.

"You have no heart," Helen stated with feigned irritation. "I'll call you in the morning and we can set up a time."

"Not too early, I haven't gotten much sleep."

"Lucky you," Helen retorted.

"Call me in the late morning," Mel repeated.

"Okay, good-bye," Helen said, and then rang off.

Mel cradled the receiver. She couldn't deny that she

wished that it had been Jim who called. She felt like a child still believing in fairy tales. He wouldn't call, and even if he wanted to, he didn't have her number.

Her eyes glanced around the dimly lit room. It was a very familiar setting, but she suddenly felt very alone. She missed him. More than she ever thought possible. It didn't make sense for the normally even-keeled person that she was. She had been correct when she told Helen that the cruise had been an eye-opener. It had turned her world upside down, and she knew that she'd never be the same.

CHAPTER FIVE

Mel stirred her white wine spritzer, tossed her swizzle stick onto the table, and frowned as she glanced at her watch. Helen was late. Her friend had warned Mel that she might be, and that wasn't what was troubling her. She was irritable and restless, and she feared that it wasn't a temporary mood. Going on the cruise had opened up a whole new world to her, one which she found both exciting and threatening. There was something very luxurious about the atmosphere on board ship, yet the trip made it difficult for her to settle back into the routine small-town life-style. Something had been left unresolved, and this gnawed at her peace of mind.

She sipped her drink as she glanced at the entrance of the small Italian restaurant. She suddenly needed to talk to her friend. She felt too close to her problem, and Helen always had a way of helping her understand what she couldn't see objectively.

Helen's pretty face appeared. She smiled and waved the instant she saw Mel. Shorter than Mel, the brunette, dressed in a navy suit and carrying a briefcase, walked swiftly toward her.

"Sorry, I'm late," Helen declared the minute she reached their table.

"That's okay, you told me you had a meeting," Mel answered with a smile.

"You look great. Rested and tanned," Helen said, setting her briefcase on the empty chair next to her.

Mel laughed. "Thanks, but I don't *feel* so rested."

Her friend gave her a skeptical glance as she sat down.

"What's the matter? Is something wrong?" she asked as concern etched her normally cheerful face.

Mel frowned as she rested her chin on her hand. Suddenly she felt vulnerable and even foolish. She had told her friend that she could handle any possible advances made by the officers. So how could she now tell her that she allowed herself to fall for the captain of the ship?

"I'm still suffering from jet lag," Mel returned, and forced a smile.

"Oh, well, that's understandable," the older woman said, signaling to the waiter.

A tall man dressed in a red mess jacket and black trousers immediately appeared. "Care for a cocktail?"

"Yes, a glass of white wine and the menus please," she stated, and glanced at her watch. "I don't have much time, but first I want to hear all about your trip," she explained.

Mel sighed. "Well, my friends were certainly right about the wolf pack. The ship wasn't even out of port when I was approached by two officers."

"I don't believe it," Helen exclaimed as her blue eyes grew bigger and her dark lashes fluttered.

"It's true, but I do have to admit that I also met some women who were looking for flings."

"You did?" Helen asked keenly.

"Yes, I was a little surprised. Perhaps I shouldn't have been, but I guess I do lead a pretty sheltered life here. Their names were Rita and Lynne, and they freely admitted that they booked the cruise only to meet men."

"That certainly gives the article objectivity."

"It certainly does," Mel agreed.

"How do you feel about writing it?"

"I could probably write a book about my experiences," Mel declared. "I'll work on my notes, and when I have them ready, I can get together with you and go over them."

"Were the men as handsome as you heard?" Helen asked with raised brows.

Just then the waiter approached their table, set Helen's drink in front of her, and handed the women menus.

Jim came instantly to mind, and Mel replied, with longing in her voice, "Yes, they were certainly handsome devils."

Her friend shot her a surprised look. Afraid that she might have given herself away, Mel smiled and casually opened her menu. "Boy, I'm starved." She stared seriously at the printed bill of fare.

Raising the large folder to cover her expression, Mel couldn't help but wonder where Jim was, and if he was on another cruise, asking some other woman for her telephone number. She knew that she would never have the answers to her questions about him, and that to ease her pain she'd better stopping asking any more.

* * *

Days passed, and Mel occupied herself with working on her article and doing repairs on her house.

Dressed in her old, faded jeans and an oversized blue and black checkered man's shirt, and holding pruning shears, Mel tackled the shrubs in front of her house. As she worked, she felt better. Working with her hands had always been therapeutic for her. She had mowed the lawn, and the aroma of freshly cut grass filled her senses. She loved that smell; it brought back so many fond memories of childhood and family.

Finally feeling a little tired, she wiped her brow and sat down on her front steps and took in her surroundings. The sun was high in a brilliant blue sky. A robin with a wiggling worm dangling from its beak flew past her and onto the limb of the old maple tree in front of her home. She wondered how old that tall, beautiful tree was. It was there some thirty years ago when her parents bought the house. Some things never change, she mused, and found comfort in that thought.

After the initial feeling of loss had passed, Mel was happy to be home. She found herself appreciating what she had taken for granted. There was contentment in the simplicity of how she lived. It wasn't that she'd forgotten about Jim. She hadn't. She accepted that what she did was the only thing she could have done and made peace with herself. But she wished that she could have handled the situation better. It had to be written off as a learning experience, and she promised herself if she should ever find herself in a similar predicament, she would confront her fears.

A dark blue car slowly pulled up in front of her house and stopped at the curb. She wondered who it was, as she didn't recognize the car, and the shrubbery blocked her view of the driver. She stood up to get a better look. The car door opened, and to her surprise Jim's large frame came into sight.

He stood for a moment, checking her mail box to make sure he had the right address. Then he turned and looked in her direction. Their eyes locked and held. A gorgeous grin spread across his face, reminding her of a blazing sunset over the Grand Canyon, and the promise of a new day that it brought. Her vow not to become involved shattered. Mel was never happier to see anyone in her whole life as she automatically waved and smiled.

Quickly they made their way toward each other.

"What are you doing here?" she asked cheerfully.

"Looking for you," he declared with a little-boy smile.

"I thought I'd never see you again," she exclaimed as she reached up to him.

He bent over and took her into his arms. The instant her breasts surged at the contact of his hard chest, Mel was brought back to reality. Regaining her composure, she pulled away. "It's marvelous to see you again!"

A mischievous glint came into his eyes, and she got the distinct feeling that he knew exactly the way she was affected by his unexpected arrival and got a kick out of it.

Her eyes narrowed as she asked, "And just *how* did you get my address?"

He glanced down at the ground, appeared to shuffle his feet, and then looked over at her steps.

"It was a long drive from the airport. Do you mind if I sit down?" he inquired casually.

"No, as long as I get the answer to my question," she retorted, placing her hands on her hips to make certain that he knew she meant business.

Without further word, he walked over to the stairs and threw himself casually into a chair. She joined him.

"You want to know how I got your address?"

She nodded.

"I looked it up in the cruise line's passenger list," he admitted in a low voice.

"What?"

"I know it was a little presumptuous of me," he declared in an apologetic tone.

"Did you say a little? That's an understatement if I ever heard one," she exclaimed.

"Well, it wasn't as if I hurt anyone. You *were* happy to see me, you must admit. So what's the harm?"

She glared at him. He would have to throw that in her face! "The harm is that I didn't want my address given out. It was personal information."

"Melanie, I can't blame you for being angry, and under normal circumstances I would never have done it. But I want to get to know you, and I didn't know how else to find you. I was proceeding on the theory that 'faint heart never won fair lady.' "

"And that gave you the right to go against my wishes?"

"If you remember, you said you didn't want me to have your phone number, but you didn't say anything about your address," he exclaimed in an appealing way.

He was trying his charm on her, and she couldn't deny that it was very effective. But a sneak was a sneak, and this sneak would be taken to task! she resolved.

"I still don't get the justification here," she exclaimed in a solemn tone.

"You were a little wary of me, and since the mountain couldn't come to Mohammed, Mohammed had to come to the mountain," he stated rationally.

Good choice of words, she thought sarcastically, but replied, "You make it sound as though you didn't do anything wrong."

Didn't the guy know when to quit? She had the goods on him, and if he was smart, he'd just admit that he was wrong.

"Melanie, I'm sorry," he suddenly said, as if in response to her unspoken words. "But you haven't heard a word I've said to you. When we met on ship, I really felt that something happened between us. Call it chemistry, call it attraction, or call it whatever you want, but I had to see you again. I wanted to know why you were attracted to me, yet when I got too close, you pushed me away. I had to find out if there was something I did or said that made you not trust me. So, when I knew that I had to be in Pittsburgh on a business deal, I decided I had to look you up. I'm going to be here only for a few days, and I would like you to have dinner with me tonight. That is, if you're free," he stated, his eyes warm and inviting.

She stared into his handsome face as she weighed his words. How convenient, she thought, not liking the thought of being squeezed in along with some financial opportunity. "So, you're here on some business deal?" she asked casually.

"Yes, I am, but don't think I wouldn't have gotten in touch with you anyway. Believe me, I would have sought you out."

"I'm glad you clarified that," she said.

"And if you don't want to see me, I promise you, I'll never bother you again," he stated earnestly.

Suddenly she thought, what had she done? She'd almost driven away forever perhaps the only man that she thought she could love. She mustn't panic, she told herself. She was in control of the situation.

There was no denying that she wanted to be with him. So why did she feel that she had to justify her emotions? She felt she had to save face, but she realized that she might lose this handsome hunk of flesh.

"So what do you say?" he asked cheerfully, pulling her out of her thoughts.

She studied him, noting his expectant expression and bright eyes, and Mel got the distinct feeling that he was a man who always got what he went after, and that persuasion was, no doubt, this man's middle name.

Suddenly memories of the cruise came back to her, and she was reminded of the article that had to be written. Seeing him again certainly gave a new twist to her story. And going out with the captain would make a good epilogue, she decided, and smiled.

"I'd love to have dinner with you," she finally declared, feeling rather sneaky herself.

"Good. You know the area better than I do. So, is there some restaurant that you've heard about, or do you have a favorite that you'd like to suggest?"

"How about Indian food?" she asked, without missing a beat.

"Terrific. Well, I'd better go to my hotel to shower and change," he exclaimed, raising his strapping frame into a standing position.

She stood up next to him, feeling very petite, and suddenly wished that she were better dressed.

"How about if I pick you up at eight?" he inquired, smiling down at her.

"Sounds good to me," she agreed. He was just too damned attractive, she thought, as her heart skipped a beat.

"See you later," he said pleasantly.

" 'Bye," she replied, and then watched him stroll confidently across her lawn and get into his car.

She stood mesmerized, not believing that he was really there. Never in her wildest dreams had she pictured him at her home. She had always been told that anticipation was greater than realization and now at last she had the opportunity of proving the adage. *Melanie,* she thought to herself, *you can work your wiles on this guy if you know what move to make, and when to make it.*

Seeing him was a good omen. She couldn't imagine why he would call on her, unless he was really telling her the truth. He cared about her and wanted to see her. But how could they possibly have a long-distance romance? It all seemed so unreal, but maybe that was the beauty of it. Her captain had come for her, she thought with a delighted chuckle.

Mel turned sharply on her heel and headed for her door. Tonight she was going to be with him, and she wanted to look her best!

Mel decided to wear one of the colorful cotton dresses that she had bought on the cruise, thinking it might be appropriate for the occasion.

Jim was prompt as he rang her buzzer exactly at eight o'clock on the button. She grabbed her white linen jacket as she rushed to the door. The minute she saw Jim, she smiled. He looked dashing, yet casual, in his dark blue blazer, silk scarf, and powder-blue shirt.

"Hello," she exclaimed as she opened the door. "Would you like to come in and have a drink first, or just go on to the restaurant?"

"I'm a bit hungry," he said. "How about you?"

She had offered to let him into her home, and he had politely refused her invitation. Now, a wolf would have cornered his prey the first chance he got, she reasoned, and thought perhaps his refusal was a good sign.

"Yes, I am, too," she uttered, with enthusiasm to match his.

He offered her his arm, which she eagerly took. Walking down a few steps in high heels, with a tall, solid man to lean on, certainly came in handy, she thought coyly.

Once seated in his car, Mel gave Jim the directions to the restaurant.

"So you flew in to the Pittsburgh airport?" she asked.

"Yes, and I rented a car and drove from there."

"Did you have any problems finding me?"

He looked over at her and smiled, then turned his attention back to the road.

"I have a funny feeling that finding you was the easy part," he said with a tinge of amusement in his voice.

"What's that supposed to mean?" she inquired, determined not to let anything get by her.

"You're a tough cookie," he exclaimed with a chuckle.

"You mean, I'm not a pushover?"

"I *never* thought you were a pushover," he quickly corrected.

"You didn't?" she asked, looking over at his profile. She wished to find some indication of what he was thinking, but his eyes were glued straight ahead and his jaw was firmly set.

"I think we're now getting to the heart of the problem," he stated.

She wanted to ask what all this "we" stuff was about, but was afraid that she would sound a little hostile. The man was starting to open up, and she didn't want to do anything that would give him the excuse not to talk, or break the mood.

"I don't understand," she said simply.

"I've done a lot of thinking about why we didn't get together. To begin with, I was going on the premise that we both wanted to. I hope I was correct," he said, glancing over at her, but didn't wait for an answer as he continued, "Then I came up with the idea that there might have been some kind of misunderstanding. That's why I came here. I wanted to talk to you to find out."

"I see," she returned in a quiet voice.

He certainly sounded sincere, and Mel was beginning to question herself as a judge of character. Could she have been that far off in her opinion of him? she wondered.

"That didn't sound very encouraging," he said. "Is this where I turn?"

"Yes, to your left," she answered, and Jim made a sharp turn.

She thought over his words. The Viking was beginning to penetrate her armor, she realized. He had traveled a good distance to talk to her, and she owed it to him and herself to set the record straight. She had enough time over the last few days to think about what had happened and what she would have liked to change.

"I know I sounded uninterested, but I was thinking. I'm glad that you are here, Jim, and that we have the opportunity to talk. I agree, we should get everything out in the open," she admitted.

Jim drove the car past the restaurant and into the parking lot. He turned off the ignition and paused before getting out. The light from the streetlight cast a shadow across his handsome face. He stared at her, his sparkling eyes telling her that he was pleased with her words.

Then as abruptly as a summer rain, he asked, "Shall we?"

She nodded, and he opened her door.

"Thank you," she said as she eased herself out of the car. She had caught the look of arousal in his eyes as he noticed the contours of her legs, but she pretended not to notice.

Closing the door after her, he glanced over at the large white structure.

"Very impressive," he declared.

"I hope you enjoy it. It's the fanciest place in town," she announced, proud of her choice.

He laughed. "Being with you, any place would be perfect."

"Thank you," she said with a slight smile playing across her lips. The silver-tongued devil was working his wiles on her, and God forbid, she was beginning to enjoy it!

Taking her hand into his larger one, he flashed her one of his boyish grins. There was something so thrilling about being at his side, she thought.

Once they were inside and seated, the owner, an older, pleasant man, said, "Hope you enjoy your dinner, Mel," and politely nodded to Jim.

Jim returned the dark-haired man's greeting, watched him leave, and then stared over at her. His look was so intense with a peculiar hue that she shifted uncomfortably in her seat.

"What's the matter? Did I grow a horn on the top of my head?" she finally asked.

"So, it's Mel, is it?" he asked, cocking a brow.

"Yes, that's what all my friends call me," she explained, thinking there was a lot about her he didn't know.

"Why didn't you tell me?"

"Because I really prefer Melanie," she replied.

But she didn't tell him that the name reminded her of family and security, and when he used her name, he gave it a special meaning.

"Okay, Melanie it is."

She smiled.

"As I said, I came to Pittsburgh to talk to a friend about some business deal," he suddenly announced.

Mel looked at him curiously. "But what about your

work? With only one month off, wouldn't it be difficult with your schedule?"

"I'm thinking of giving up the sea altogether and changing jobs entirely."

"You are?"

"Yes, I'll be giving up some money and the glamour of being a captain, but I'm ready for a change," he stated.

"Really?" she asked, surprised.

"I guess you didn't believe me when I told you I was getting bored," he stated with penetrating eyes.

"I suppose I didn't," she admitted.

"Well, it's true. And I might be making quite a few trips to Pittsburgh in the near future. Could you handle that?"

"Why couldn't I?" she asked, wondering what he was implying.

"Do you always answer a question with a question?"

"Depends on the question," she retorted, not giving an inch.

"I hoped you would be happy about it," he stated.

Just then the dining room captain appeared as if on cue at their table.

"Good evening, sir. May I order some cocktails for you and madame? Or perhaps you would prefer some wine. Of course, you may order anything you like, but, as you know, we specialize in Indian food. The chicken curry with wild rice is very appetizing. We serve it with Major Grey's Chutney and herbs, and a Waldorf salad."

"That sounds great. Melanie, shall we try it?" Jim asked.

"Yes, I'll join you," Mel answered as she smiled, thinking what a shrewd and thoughtful man the dining room captain was. She had heard his spiel on several occasions with different dates, and he never let on to Jim that she had.

"May I suggest a glass of Chablis, or perhaps a bottle, sir?" the captain asked.

"Shall I order a bottle?" Jim inquired.

"Why not, if you want to," Mel declared.

"Shall I bring you the wine list, sir?"

"No, that won't be necessary, the Chablis will do," Jim returned.

"Thank you," the man answered, and swiftly departed.

"You didn't ask me if I'd be happy about seeing you, Jim," Mel said, resuming their conversation. "You asked me if I could handle seeing you. There is a difference, you know," she explained.

"Okay, how do you feel? Are you happy to know that I might be around?" he inquired sheepishly.

"Yes, I am. Can you handle that?" she asked playfully.

"*Touché,*" he came back, and laughed. "Well, I'm glad that's settled. Because, I'm planning to see a lot of you," he admitted.

"That sounds like a threat," she said with a laugh.

"No, but it's a promise."

A silence came over them as their eyes locked and held. The blood came to her cheeks as she experienced the strongest desire to be in his arms. Then she smiled mysteriously.

"Now it's my turn—what's so funny?" he asked with curious eyes.

"I just never pictured myself sitting here with you. It's as if we could be anywhere . . ."

Her voice trailed off, and she laughed nervously.

"You probably don't know what I'm talking about, and probably think I'm crazy," she stated wistfully.

"Try me," he encouraged.

She leaned back in her chair and folded her hands. "To put it simply, I'm very glad that you are here."

"Thank you. I feel the same," he admitted, and touched her hand.

His gesture was so gentle that it had unlocked her heart and soul. And she knew that she wanted to be with this man, longed to experience him, and knew that if he wanted her, she would be with him. At that very moment, nothing else mattered.

He suddenly smiled. Each time she saw him, the pull was stronger, and she no longer had the energy to resist him. Nor did she feel the need to. She was in her own territory and in control. She also realized that she was probably a little in love with him. She had sat in this same restaurant a dozen times, but sitting next to him was pure magic.

After the waiter served the wine, Jim raised his glass in salute, and tapping her glass, he toasted, "To us!"

Mel smiled, nodded, and sipped her wine.

"I like Adamsville," he said.

"You do?"

"Yes, it reminds me of the town where I grew up," he explained.

"You said you lived in Philadelphia."

"I do, but I was raised in a small town outside of there."

"So, we have another thing in common," she exclaimed.

A puzzled expression crossed his face as he asked, "What's the first thing?"

She laughed. "How quickly we forget! Mysteries, remember?"

An embarrassed look came into his eyes. "Of course I do. I was just too taken by your beauty to think straight."

"You could talk your way out of a paper bag if you had to," she teased.

"I know I had a job to do and I was pretty busy on the ship. But I want to know why you evaded me," he stated with a sudden serious expression.

What could she tell him? That he was just too damned attractive, and that she hadn't trusted him? No, she didn't particularly want to say that.

"Evade isn't exactly the word. I found you attractive, but I questioned your motives," she stated.

The instant the words were out of her mouth, she felt better, as if a weight had been lifted from her shoulders.

"Thank you, Melanie, for being honest. I can understand and appreciate your caution. After what I've seen on some of my cruises, I question why any woman would even want to be on a ship alone, unless, of course, she was looking for a fling."

Mel shot him a skeptical glance.

Jim laughed softly. "Don't get me wrong, I wasn't referring to you. I did wonder why you traveled alone, but I decided that you weren't the type. Besides, I gave you a few opportunities to seduce me, but you let a good thing slip through your fingers," he teased.

Boy, he was certainly feeling his oats, she mused.

"The night's not over yet," she suddenly blurted out, and covered her remark with laughter.

He studied her, his expression serious. She had not gotten the laugh that she had expected. It felt more as if she'd just stepped on a rattler's nest.

"I want to be with you, Melanie, I can't deny that, but only if it's right."

"And how do you know when it's right?" she asked boldly.

"You'll know," he returned, and took some of his drink.

She sat back in her chair. Did he mean that he would wait until she wanted him? That was gentlemanly, but she hoped that he didn't expect her to make the first move. That would be a little difficult, especially after the way she had resisted him in the past.

"Isn't that the way you like it?" Jim challenged.

"I think for a man who likes to be direct, we're skirting the issue a bit," she retorted, knowing that she sounded ridiculous.

Jim raised his brow as his eyes narrowed. "Okay, I want to make love to you, but I would never force myself on you. I want you to want me."

Why did conversations about sex with men always make her a little nervous? For some reason, she always thought that it wasn't something a person talked about, but just did.

"I can tell this conversation is making you a little uneasy. Let's change the subject," he suggested kindly.

"Thank you."

Mel glanced down at her hands folded in her lap. To

108

her relief, the waiter suddenly appeared with their salads, and she realized how hungry she was. As the man placed their plates in front of them, Mel glanced over at Jim and he smiled at her. Whom was he kidding? The man had to know how much she already wanted him. Every time he looked at her that way, her heart melted.

It was dark, but a full moon lit up the sky as they walked across her cricket-serenaded lawn. Mel was pondering whether she should chance it for the second time that day and ask him in when they made their way up her steps.

But before she came to any decision, Jim had taken matters into his own hands and flopped into one of the chairs on the porch.

"That was a wonderful choice of restaurants," he complimented.

"I'm glad that you liked it." She sat in a chair next to him.

"So, when are you going to take your next cruise?" he asked.

Mel laughed. *"That* will be the last ship ride for me for a while!"

Jim gave her a skeptical glance. "I don't understand you. You told me you had a good time, but you talk as if you'd escaped from Alcatraz."

"Well, I had been warned about the wolf pack, and I found out about it myself."

"I do hope that you're only talking about Mr. West," he said with a cocked brow.

"Oh, I'm sorry, I should have clarified that," she teased.

"He certainly was smitten with you," he admitted.

And Jim certainly had him shaking in his boots, she wanted to say, but bit her tongue.

"You were pretty popular yourself," she retorted.

"All in the line of duty," he quipped. "I hope I can see you tomorrow night."

"Yes, I would like to see you, too," she answered immediately.

He glanced at his watch and quickly stood up. "Sorry for being so abrupt, but I do have an early meeting tomorrow, and I know you should get your beauty rest," he said fondly.

Mel stood up and immediately wondered if he would try his kiss on her again. She hoped that he would. It was kind of exciting crumpling in his wonderfully powerful arms.

He bent over, and she closed her eyes. To her surprise, his lips brushed lightly across her forehead. It was a sweet, gentle kiss, and it meant the world to her. Before she knew it, he was gone, and she slid back down into her seat.

She thought about their evening together. She had flirted with him, yet tried to make mental notes of what they said. She was beginning to trust him, yet there was a doubt. She wondered what lengths a man like Jim would go to, to get what he wanted. And just maybe she did have a new slant to her article—about how one particular officer jumped ship to track down his quarry.

CHAPTER SIX

The minute daylight crept into her bedroom window, Mel was awakened. Jim came instantly to mind. She had to admit that seeing him turned her world upside down. But it was a wonderful omen for the future. A change for the better, she thought happily.

She turned onto her side, thinking that she'd sleep a little longer. But after a few moments, she was too stimulated, so she got out of her brass bed and walked over to the window and held back the lacy white curtain. The chirping birds were all that could be heard and the grass still glistened with the early-morning dew. Later, she would be seeing her captain, and all was right with the world.

A soft smile curled up the corners of her lips, and she released the curtain. Turning, she decided to begin writing her article. She had already collated her notes and made an outline. She would be meeting Helen in a few days and thought she'd surprise her friend with a few pages of her story.

Grabbing her robe, she walked with an air of purpose toward her study. But as she moved, she couldn't help hoping that the day would pass quickly as she anxiously looked forward to seeing Jim again.

* * *

Sitting across from him in a dimly lit, intimate restaurant, Mel couldn't believe how restless she was.

As the waiter cleared away their dinner dishes, Mel unconsciously played with her spoon.

"Why are you so nervous?" Jim asked, catching her off guard.

Slightly embarrassed, she smiled politely. "I don't know."

He looked at her with concern. How could she admit that every nerve in her body was alive and tingling, and that she was in the state of unappeased desire? Her arousal had almost reached the point that if she weren't in his arms soon, she'd jump him right there at the table.

Suddenly their eyes met and the moment of truth arrived. The expression in his eyes responded to her longing, and she was filled with the thought that she was about to experience the greatest adventure of her life.

"What do you say we get out of here and go to my hotel?" he asked with a mischievous glint in his eyes.

Mel laughed. The devil had echoed her own sentiments!

"I thought you'd never ask," she retorted brazenly.

He flashed her his enigmatic smile and immediately signaled the waiter.

The trip was a speedy one. Mel never remembered her feet hitting the sidewalk, nor Jim starting the car. Her emotions were in the state of uncertainty, numbing everything around her. It was as though she had been transported onto a cloud, being carried off to some fantasy kingdom as Pluto made off with Persephone. And she was going willingly, giving herself over to her Viking.

Before she knew it, she was in his hotel room and into his arms. His lips reached down and claimed hers, sending a scorching bolt of electricity through her. Her body responded with a tremor as she wrapped her arms around him and returned his kiss with all her heart. His eager tongue parted her lips and explored every crevice of her mouth.

Moments passed, but time stood still as she swayed under his magnetic power. His strong body pressed against hers, and she felt a strength she had never known. For the first time in her life, she wanted to be swept away by her emotions without weighing whether she was doing the right thing. She wanted to be with him more than she had ever wanted to be with anyone, and no longer cared about his motives.

Suddenly he took his sensual lips from hers, and she instantly stared into his flushed face. The misty vulnerability in his eyes was almost painful to see. Could this rugged, worldly captain be experiencing the same kind of longing and desire that she was at this very moment? She didn't think it possible, but his expression warned her that she just might be wrong.

Without uttering a word, he reached up and gently unbuttoned the top of her blouse. He slid his hand inside and cupped the aroused nipples of her breasts.

"God, you're so lovely," he moaned, tenderly massaging her.

"Oh, Jim!" she exclaimed. "Please, make love to me!" she pleaded.

Immediately he helped her out of her linen jacket and then effortlessly lifted her into his arms and carried her over to the bed. Setting her carefully down, he knelt beside her as a strange, indefinable look came into his eyes.

"I've dreamed of making love to you, Melanie, but now that I'm actually with you, I feel as if this is a dream," he said with a soft chuckle.

She automatically reached over and stroked the side of his head. "I know, darling. It's hard for me to believe that I'm finally with you. Words can't express how much I want you," she admitted in a husky, silken tone.

Her words pleased him, and he bent over and kissed the tip of her nose.

She laughed, the sound a release of all her pent-up emotions.

As he watched her, she slowly began to undress. As she removed her white linen blouse, his expression told her that he liked what he saw. Their eyes met and held. A mystical, sensual light passed between them sending her pulse racing. As if he understood her urgency, he began to undress.

The instant their bodies touched, a wave of pleasure washed over her.

"I've waited so long," he whispered, stroking her soft ivory shoulders.

"Forever," she exclaimed in a passion-laden voice.

He took her into his strong arms and her breasts surged as they felt his hard, manly chest. She hugged him to her as his lips swooped down to her mouth, pressing against her lips feverishly. He kissed her cheek, her forehead, and then the tip of her nose.

"I like that pert little nose of yours," he said playfully.

"I gathered that," she came back happily.

A serious look came into his eyes as his hand caressed her breast, teasing her taut nipple.

"But that's not all I like," he exclaimed in a voice choked with emotion.

He lowered his head as he kissed her pink aroused bud. And Mel thought that she had surely died and gone to heaven with a smile upon her face as her body exploded with ecstasy.

Suddenly he released her swollen breast and peered down at her. He smiled. Softly his breath fanned her face.

"Let me look at you," he whispered.

His words delighted her as she heard the desire in his voice. A delicious shudder heated her body.

His gaze dropped from her eyes to her shoulders to her breasts. Then he gently eased her onto her back. Slowly and seductively, his gaze slid downward. His hand softly moved across her stomach as his lips followed its trail. Electricity seemed to arc through her, and all thoughts fragmented as his hands and lips continued their hungry search of her body.

Finally no longer able to harness her need of him, she cried out, "Love me, darling," and her hands swung out wildly, urging him to her. "I want you, I need you!"

In answer to her plea, he raised himself over her. For a brief moment he stared down at her. She suddenly sensed her own frailty. His look was penetrating, as though he could see clear through to her very soul. Was he basking in his power over her, or was he so carried away by the emotion of the moment?

With one expert thrust, he entered her. She abandoned herself to the whirl of sensation as Mel was sent on a wonderfully maddening journey. Never in her life had she experienced such excitement and never in her life had she ever given herself so completely.

As their bodies moved in unison, a fury overcame them. His drive was relentless as he thrilled her beyond belief. Her body tensed as her breath came in long, surrendering moans of erotic pleasure. Suddenly she gasped in sweet agony as Jim joined her and exploded with a fire of his own. Her body went limp and melted into his. His heart thudded against her chest as their glistening bodies lay entwined. She was filled with an amazing sense of completeness.

Moments passed as they held each other. His breathing finally came in slow, even breaths, and he gently eased himself off her. Instantly she felt her separateness.

Looking over at her, he smiled. A look as proud as a peacock came into his eyes. "Was it worth the wait?" he asked mischievously.

"I think you know the answer to that one, Captain!"

He reached over and caressed her breast, rekindling a smoldering fire. He flashed her one of his easy smiles as he exclaimed confidently, "You haven't seen anything yet."

Mel's curiosity was heightened by this remark, and she looked forward to the demonstration.

"After all," she said, "the proof of the pudding is in the eating."

He possessively captured her breast with his mouth as his tongue toyed with its excited nipple. A tremor heated her thighs and groin as she impulsively reached over and touched him. She caressed him gently and her heart was filled with love as she experienced his response to her. His lips urgently found hers, and she was thrilled by his desire for her. Their lovemaking began anew as they exploded with a passion beyond all expectation. Mel was carried on a more exciting journey than she ever imagined possible. She was with the man she loved, and it was even more incredible than her rational mind could ever fathom.

The following morning, curled next to Jim, Mel's body was satisfied, but her mind troubled. She had allowed herself to be seduced by her captain and now didn't feel very good about it. He might be out of her life in a few days, and instead of wondering what she had missed, she knew what she would be missing. Making love to Jim was an incredible experience, out of this world. But she felt guilty about her original motive for going to dinner with him. During both dates, she had felt like two people: one who had flirted and enjoyed his company, and the other who had been cool and calculating, trying to assemble facts for her article.

Jim suddenly stirred next to her and reached over to hug her. Mel instinctively pretended to be asleep. Time was needed to sort out her emotions. A sadness ripped through her heart. To be touched so completely by another human being and have him then disappear from her life would be very painful for her.

Jim got out of bed and walked toward the bathroom. As she heard the sound of the door closing and then the shower, she moved over to the spot where Jim had lain and hugged his pillow.

Moments passed before he came back into the room. A drawer was opened and closed. Finally the inevitable happened. He came around to her side of the bed and gently shook her.

"I'm sorry, Melanie, to wake you, but I have to be leaving soon for my appointment. Would you like to stay here, or shall I take you home?" he asked in a soft voice.

Mel opened her eyes. The scent of lime aftershave filled her senses. He was standing over her with the most loving eyes she had ever seen. His hair was still damp and he wore a white shirt. A yellow silk tie dangled loosely from around his neck, waiting to be tied, and his gray trousers were very becoming.

A smile graced her lips. "I'm getting up," she answered groggily.

He chuckled softly.

"What's so funny?" she inquired.

"You. I think I've got one hell of a satisfied woman on my hands," he exclaimed playfully.

"When you're right, you're right." She sat up at the edge of the bed.

"I must look a wreck," she suddenly announced.

"You look beautiful," he stated.

She stared into his eyes and saw the reflection of his words.

"Thank you," she uttered, and moved to get out of bed.

But he quickly sat next to her and put his arms around her. Mel's head rested against his hard chest, and wondered when he would be leaving.

"You're an incredibly sexy lady," he exclaimed.

"You're not so bad yourself," she teased.

"You're lucky that I have to go to a meeting."

118

"I think you've got that the other way around," she stated with a laugh.

"Boy, did you fool me on the ship!" he said in a disbelieving way.

"What's that supposed to mean?"

He chuckled. "You had me so confused that I began to wonder whether you had a problem with your sexuality."

"I'm so glad we got that cleared up," she said.

"Me too."

He looked at his watch.

"I know, it's time to go," she moaned.

"All good things have to come to an end—for a while," he said warmly, and then ran his fingers gently through her hair.

He kissed her forehead and then rose. Mel carefully stood up. A headache threatened, and she didn't want Jim to know how she really felt. She gathered up her clothes and walked toward the bathroom to get dressed.

As the car stopped in front of her home, Mel insisted that Jim needn't walk her to her door.

"I'm fine. You're late and you better get going," she exclaimed.

"Sure?" he questioned with concerned eyes.

"Positive."

"All right, but I'll be back early, and we'll have dinner."

"Great."

He smiled and kissed her. She smiled in return as she got out of his car. He waved, and she waved back. She stood on the curb until his car was out of sight.

Slowly she turned and walked across her lawn toward her house.

Once inside, she hurried to her bedroom and flung herself across her bed. She didn't know whether to cry or yell. With the dawn, she had been hurtled back to earth as reality struck. It was hard for her to believe that he had actually looked her up. The man was just so damned more worldly than she, and this bothered Mel. And the worst part was, she was falling in love with him.

She had to talk to someone. She needed to get her feelings into perspective. Her friend Helen would be the perfect choice to speak to. She was always giving Mel good advice and would know what to do.

Moments passed as Mel wondered what she could tell her friend. She hoped that Helen wouldn't think her a little deceitful for not telling her in the first place. She could understand if she did, but after Mel explained to her why she hadn't mentioned Jim, Helen would surely understand. Besides, Mel wanted her to meet Jim. That way, Helen would be able to give her good insight into the man. Her friend understood men better than she, and could calm or confirm her fears about him.

Without further ado, Mel jumped up from the bed and headed for the phone. She would ask Helen to join them for cocktails, but would meet her a little earlier so the two women could talk before Jim joined them. After Mel dialed Helen's number and extended the invitation, Helen said she would be delighted to meet Jim, but Mel hadn't missed the surprise in her friend's voice.

Feeling a little better, Mel decided it was about time

that she took a shower. She glanced at her reflection in her bathroom mirror. She couldn't believe that she'd allowed the man of her dreams to see her in such a condition. Her face looked tired, but no one could deny the rosy glow in her cheeks. She automatically smiled as she recalled their wild evening of lovemaking. What surprised her more than anything was her own driving need. It was as if all of her inhibitions had been broken down when she was in his arms. She wondered what spell he had woven over her. Whatever it was, it was thrilling beyond all belief.

She sighed and began to undress.

Later, Mel sat next to Helen in one of their favorite casual spots in town. Jim had called her earlier that day, and she asked him if he would like to meet Helen. He was pleased that she wanted to introduce him to her friend and asked where they were to meet.

Helen raised her glass and took a sip. Setting the glass on the table, she turned to Mel. "Well, how long are you going to hold me in suspense?" she asked coyly.

"I wondered when that was coming!" Mel shot back.

"I sensed there was something other than jet lag troubling you when we met for lunch. But I knew you'd tell me when you were ready," Helen answered, raising her dark eyebrows.

"I felt like an idiot, telling you that I could handle the men on board, and then I go and fall for the captain of the ship! I'm sorry that I didn't confide in you. It was just that I really felt too vulnerable and really didn't understand my own feelings, much less try to explain them to you," Mel said, and sipped her drink.

"You don't owe me an explanation," Helen exclaimed. "We're friends."

"Well, I still feel like an idiot," Mel stated.

"Tell me about this guy. You said he was the captain."

"Yes," Mel returned with a laugh.

"If you're going to fall it might as well be for the top banana," Helen teased.

"I knew you would have a way of putting this all into perspective," Mel retorted, feigning a frown.

"Okay, so you want me to be a little more serious."

Mel sipped her Bloody Mary, set it on the table, and ran her finger up the cool side of the glass. "I'm crazy about the man, and I may never see him again," she admitted.

"What?"

"Well, he said that he might be in Pittsburgh for business, but I don't know. I made love to him last night and now I wish that I hadn't."

"I don't understand."

"I don't either," Mel admitted, shaking her head.

"Are you saying that you don't think he cares about you?" Helen inquired gently.

Mel sighed. "I suppose so. I was so attracted to him on the cruise and I wanted to be with him, but I resisted, afraid that he was like the officers I would be writing about. And I really thought that he was. When I left the ship, I was saddened because I knew that I'd wonder what I had missed. But when he showed up at my doorstep, I instantly fell into his arms."

"I see. So, now you're wondering how you could

122

have such different opinions about the same man. And are afraid that your emotions for him allowed you to be swept away by the passion of the moment?"

"Something like that."

"You're questioning your judgment?"

"Yes, that's why I wanted you to meet him. Maybe you can see what I can't see," she exclaimed.

Helen raised her glass and thought a moment before tasting the liquid. "I hope I can be of help, Mel," she said earnestly.

"I know."

Just then Mel suddenly sensed that Jim was near. Before she turned to look, she knew he was there.

"I think Jim's here," she quickly told Helen in a hushed voice.

The women both stared over at the entrance to the restaurant.

He smiled and waved the moment he spotted them.

As he strolled toward them, Helen said in a low voice, "I can certainly see his appeal. He's a very striking man."

"Yes, I thought so, too," Mel murmured.

Upon reaching their table, he said, "Hi, Melanie, and Helen?"

"Yes, I'm Helen," she responded as she extended her hand.

Jim shook it warmly before he seated himself between the two women.

"Hello, there," he said, smiling over at Mel.

"Hi, yourself," she returned pleasantly.

Jim glanced around the restaurant, taking in the packed tables. "This is a comfortable little place," he exclaimed.

"Yes, it's one of our favorites," Mel said, including Helen.

"Ah, so now I know your watering hole," he said with a chuckle.

"Oh, we've got plenty of other pit stops," Helen said mischievously.

Jim cocked one brow. "You two have a lot in common," he stated playfully.

Mel laughed, and Helen shot her a surprised look.

"He thinks I'm a tough cookie," Mel explained.

"Well, he's right about that," Helen exclaimed with a laugh.

Jim smiled and then signaled the waiter. "Are you ready for another drink? Name your poison," he retorted as the waiter approached.

"That's ship lingo," Mel teased as she smiled over at Jim. "Would you like another drink, Helen?"

"No, not just yet."

"I'm fine, too," Mel admitted.

"Then give me a Scotch and soda," he said to the waiter.

"Thank you," the man returned, and took off.

"I suppose Melanie told you that she met me on the cruise," he said, addressing Helen.

"Yes, she did."

"Did she tell you that I had to follow her all the way to your little town?" he asked.

"You did?" Helen inquired evasively.

"Yes, I did. Do you work with her?" he suddenly asked.

"No, I don't," Helen answered, and Mel instantly tensed.

The article came sharply to mind, and she had forgotten to tell her friend not to mention it to the captain.

"Oh, I thought that's how you became friends," he stated.

"No, we grew up together. I'm an editor for a local magazine," she explained.

Mel downed her drink. "Jim, excuse me, but I think I would like another one." She indicated her empty glass.

"Certainly," he said, immediately catching the waiter's attention.

Helen gave her a skeptical glance, and Mel hoped that her friend understood her intention.

After Jim gave the waiter Mel's drink order, he turned back to Helen.

"I'd love to read one of your issues sometime," he declared.

"Fine, I'll get your address from Mel and send you one."

"No, you don't have to do that. I'm going to move here," he said, taking Mel's hand in his.

"You definitely are?" Mel asked with surprise.

"Yes, and I think we should celebrate tonight," he announced.

"That sounds wonderful," Helen stated, smiling over at Mel with a mischievous look to her eyes.

Mel couldn't help but laugh. "I think so, too," she retorted, squeezing Jim's big hand.

The evening wore on as the threesome chatted and laughed a lot. Finally when dinnertime arrived, Helen rose and said that it was time for her to leave. Jim and Mel insisted that she stay, but she stubbornly refused.

Taking her leave, she politely shook Jim's hand and winked to Mel before she exited.

"She really cares about you," Jim said the moment Helen was out of earshot.

"Yes, I know, and I care about her."

"I'm glad you have a friend like that."

"Thank you."

"Don't mention it," he said playfully.

"You're in a good mood," she commented.

"Yes, it's because I'm with my favorite lady."

"Favorite out of how many?"

"How about one out of one?"

"And what about that blonde I saw you with on the ship?" she asked brazenly.

Jim raised his shoulders sheepishly and laughed. "I wondered when you would get around to her," he said with amusement.

"You did, did you?"

"Yes, I did," he returned confidently.

"And what about the little exchange of numbers?" she asked with narrowed eyes.

"Correction—exchange of a number."

"So, you did get her telephone number!" she fumed.

"Melanie, what am I supposed to do if a woman comes up and gives me her number? I'm supposed to be host of a floating hotel. My job is to entertain . . ."

"And keep all the women happy," she interrupted.

"There's only one woman I want to keep happy and that's you," he said softly, a seriousness coming into his eyes.

He certainly knew how to say all the right words, she thought as she smiled.

"Now, tell me about your new job," she demanded.

"Give me a kiss first," he said in a boyish way.

Mel looked around to see if anyone was looking. Satisfied that they weren't, she leaned over and planted a big one on his lips.

"Thanks, I needed that," he said with a grin.

"Tell me about your job," she insisted.

"Did anyone ever tell you that you had a one-track mind?"

"Get on with it," she ordered with a laugh.

"The most important part is that I'm going to be near you. I've decided to go ahead with forming a new business venture with my friend. It's a security engineering business. I would go in and check the safety of the ship. There would be a lot of travel involved in the work, but not as long a period of time as being captain of a ship."

"That sounds great," she declared.

"I'm ready for a change. And I want to get to know you more to see where this could go," he stated with warm, loving eyes.

"I don't understand."

"Hey, I hoped you didn't think I was just a one-night stand. I'm talking long-range plans here," he admitted openly.

Mel was afraid to believe what he was saying was true, but she did suddenly feel a lot better. Perhaps she should just relax and see what he did.

"How long have you known about moving around here?" she inquired.

"Just before I met you," he stated casually.

Her brows raised. "You did?" she asked with surprise.

"Yes," he returned, and Mel lowered her gaze, staring down at the white tablecloth. Then, on the ship, the captain might have been telling her the truth, and she couldn't believe how foolish she suddenly felt.

"Well, I think it's wonderful news, Jim. You *certainly* surprised me," she stated.

"That was the plan," he said, pleased with himself, but he had failed to notice the tinge of sarcasm in her voice.

He reached over and took her hand in his. She forced a smile.

Here she had been taking all the blame for their not getting together, when he had held back a bit of information that would have made a big difference to her.

A waiter handed them menus.

"I'm hungry," she declared as her eyes glanced over the entrées.

"So am I," Jim agreed.

Mel could hardly see the printed words, her mind riveted on her revelation. Had he told her that he might be living near her, his asking for her number would have made sense. She still might have questioned his motives, but she possibly would have given him her number on the premise that time would tell what the captain was really made of. So why hadn't he told her his plans? Didn't he know that would have helped her trust him a little more?

"What do you think you're going to have?" Jim asked, suddenly pulling her out of her thoughts.

"I don't know. How about you?" she quickly asked.

"Probably the filet mignon."

"Sounds good."

"Why don't you have one, too?"

"Okay," she stated pleasantly. Closing the menu and setting it on the table, she looked at Jim.

His expression was so adorable, so vulnerable, as he grinned, that she didn't have the heart to continue on with this disquieting line of mental dialogue. It was best that she let it be, she reasoned. They were happy, life was sweet. So why cause any ripples on the peaceful stream? She automatically touched Jim's hand.

He smiled, wrapped his hand around hers. "Glad you're back," he said softly.

He seemed to know her so well, she thought, and admitted, "Me, too," very pleased to be with this wonderful man.

Mel lay curled in her brass bed, wrapped in Jim's thrilling arms, feeling totally satisfied. It had been a big decision to bring him home to make love. Before, going to his hotel room had seemed like the perfect answer to not being left with memories of him in the place where she lived when he disappeared out of her life. But now she had been given hope of a bright future. He would be around, and she had the chance to find out if her captain was for real.

He gently caressed her breast as a delightful tingling coursed through her spine, and she felt him, hard and aroused against her thigh. His immediate response to her delighted her. She couldn't believe how incredibly sexy she felt with this man. It wasn't that she hadn't made love before. But she had never experienced such completeness, such total oneness with the world, and such power over a man.

The strong need to be a part of him overcame her, and she turned to face him. Her lips sought his as he kissed her with a passion that matched hers. He roughly crushed her to his chest, and her legs wildly wrapped themselves around his, bringing him in closer to her, as every fiber in her body cried out for release.

Jim rolled onto his back, pulling her up on top of him. As she straddled this handsome, virile man, a beautiful, heart-rending look came into his eyes. He reached up and gently squeezed her breasts. His touch was pure magic, and waves of ecstasy rippled through her.

"You're my one and only, my precious angel," he moaned.

He had spoken the words she longed to hear, and she cried happily, "My darling!"

Instantly he entered her, and she welcomed him, her body blazing with a fanatic fire, bursting into a million brilliant flames. Their bodies exploded in a frenzy of abandonment, and Mel could have sworn that she felt the earth turn on its axis.

His words, that he cared about her, kept ringing through her mind, driving her on to unbelievable heights of joy.

CHAPTER SEVEN

The next morning Mel watched as Jim slipped on his shoes. Sitting next to him on the bed, she couldn't dismiss the dull ache inside. She had tried to be brave and cheerful, not wanting him to know how badly she felt about his leaving. And she knew it was foolish of her to be so emotional about it. He had reassured her that he only had to tie up some loose ends on his job, and would be back with her as soon as was humanly possible. But she couldn't help but feel that everything was too perfect, too incredible, and that something was bound to go wrong. Together she felt they were an unbeatable force, but alone, she questioned their vulnerability.

"You look so sad, Melanie," Jim stated with concern.

She suddenly realized that she had allowed to let her mask drop, and he had seen the worry behind it.

"I'm going to miss you," she stated simply. What else was there to say? It wasn't right for her to let him leave, knowing her fears.

Jim sighed and put his arm around her. "It's that time," he announced wearily.

"I know," she murmured.

"I care a lot about you," he said.

"You know how I feel about you, too."

He kissed her tenderly on the forehead.

"You make me a very happy man," he whispered as his warm breath fanned her cheek.

"I'm glad," she returned in a barely audible voice.

Her last words were smothered on his lips as she kissed him good-bye.

"Thanks, I needed that," he said, his eyes warm.

"Now, you'd better get going or you'll miss your plane," she said more cheerfully than she felt.

"I still have a few minutes," he insisted, looking over at her clock radio.

"The sooner you leave, the sooner you'll come back," she said.

She couldn't bear for him to see the tears welling up in her eyes. This was difficult for her, and she couldn't stand any long-drawn-out good-byes.

"I think you're trying to get rid of me," he stated, feigning a hurt expression.

Mel laughed. "That's a good one. I'm not the one who's leaving!"

A seriousness came over him. "Melanie, I don't want to leave you. I'll be back soon," he said earnestly.

"I know," she answered, as they simultaneously stood up.

Arm in arm they walked through her house, out onto the porch, and down the steps.

As they stood on her lawn, Jim said, "I'll call you as soon as I get to Fort Lauderdale."

"I'll be expecting your call," she said, her voice already filled with expectation.

He bent over and kissed her softly, and then turned to leave.

Mel stood shaking as he disappeared out of her world. She hardly remembered him leaving, but the emptiness that she felt reminded her that he had.

After a few moments, she turned and walked toward her house.

He told her that he was coming back, so why did she feel so badly? she wondered. Was she intuitively responding to something she didn't know about yet? She didn't like that thought, and she immediately knew that she had to talk to Helen. Not only were they to discuss the article today, but she needed to find out what her friend thought of Jim. It was easy for her to lose herself in his arms, but now that he was gone, everything was a muddle, and she needed her friend's objectivity. With that thought in mind, Mel's feet gained momentum and carried her swiftly in the direction of her phone.

"This is actually quite good!" Helen declared, pleased, as she looked over Mel's first pages of the article.

"You really like them?" Mel asked with surprise.

Helen was an extremely talented editor and also quite selective, which made Mel doubly appreciate her words.

"I wouldn't say so if it weren't true," she replied, resting her hands on the table. "Just a few minor corrections, that's all."

"Well, I'm very happy to hear that!" Mel said, beaming.

"Now, let's get down to the real problem," Helen stated with a knowing look as her voice deepened.

"You always have a way of cutting right through to the heart of the matter, don't you?" Mel inquired with a laugh.

"That's why I'm so good at what I do," she retorted without missing a beat.

"I can't argue with that," Mel agreed, and took a sip of her coffee. "Where shall I begin?"

"At the beginning," her friend encouraged.

Mel sighed. "I don't want to bore you with all that again, but the minute Jim left, I had mixed feelings about being with him."

"I don't understand."

"He says that he's going to live around here, and I'm really happy about that. But I can't help wondering whether I allowed myself to get involved with him too quickly."

Helen drank her coffee and studied her friend as though she were going over Mel's words. "I think the guy is crazy about you. I really don't feel that Jim is the typical man on the make. Why would he come all this way?"

"Business."

"I suppose anything is possible, but I think he really cares for you. I saw that special look in his eyes whenever he looks at you."

"Well, I value your opinion, Helen. You're a pretty good judge of character, so I hope you're right."

"This must be serious."

Mel stared over into her friend's dark eyes, wondering what her implication was.

"You've had boyfriends before, and you could always take them or leave them, but this one . . ."

Helen's words dropped off as her hands and eyebrows were raised simultaneously.

Mel smiled. "Yes, this one is different. I think I'm in love with the guy."

"Now everything is clear."

"What do you mean?"

"Obviously you're experiencing the 'first-time jitters,' that's all," her friend exclaimed.

"Oh, that explains everything," Mel responded, giving her a frustrated look.

"What I mean, Mel, is that it's natural to question yourself and him. This is all very new to you, and it can be a little scary at first. I just better be your maid of honor, that's all!" she said with a chuckle.

"Cute!" Mel retorted.

"Relax, everything will be fine. You both care about each other, so you don't have anything to worry about," Helen reassured her.

Mel sighed and then smiled. "I do feel better, and I suppose you're right. He's going to call me tonight," she announced as her face brightened.

"Just take one step at a time, and it'll work out."

"Thanks, Helen. I don't know what I'd do without a friend like you."

"You'd be fine, that's what."

Mel smiled. She felt very lucky to have Helen as a friend, and she was right about taking it easy. Nothing ever worked when a person worked too hard at it. Suddenly she was ravenous, and glanced at her watch to see what time it was. Satisfied that she would be home early enough to get Jim's call, she thought she'd like to get some dinner before she went home.

"I know we said that we were only going to meet for

coffee, but I *am* hungry, and I wondered if you wanted to have some dinner here with me?"

"Yes, if you have time."

"Absolutely," Mel said.

By the time dinner was finished and Mel was on her way home, she felt great. She had had a wonderful visit with her friend, Helen liked what she had done on the article, and Jim would be talking to her tonight. What more could a woman want? she mused as she drove her beige station wagon into her garage. Turning off the ignition, she stepped out of the car and pulled down the garage door. She glanced up at the dark clouds covering the full moon, and she remembered that the forecast was for rain tomorrow. But that didn't dampen her spirits. She would spend the day inside, going through all her business magazines and periodicals, reading some and throwing some out, and perhaps start on the pair of antique chairs that she'd been wanting to refurbish.

As she walked into the house, she decided to pour herself a glass of sherry. That done, she picked up her mystery and decided to finish the last two chapters. She curled into her father's old leather chair and set her drink on the small wooden table next to the phone. Contented, she began to read.

Minutes passed and she glanced at her watch. Perhaps he had called earlier when she was out with Helen, and she had missed his call. But surely he would call back, she reasoned, and took a sip of sherry. Maybe he had tried to reach her in the morning when she was talking on the phone, she suddenly thought, and he couldn't get through. But her line hadn't been busy all day, she reminded herself.

Setting the glass down, she sighed and picked up the book again. She wanted to finish it and was determined to concentrate. Helen's words, "relax, and everything will be fine," came sharply to mind, and Mel automatically smiled. Just because she hadn't heard from him yet, she was beginning to think the worst. How foolish, she thought, and glanced immediately down at the page.

But by eleven o'clock she slammed the book closed. She had finished it, it was late, and her phone still hadn't rung. How strange of him not to try to reach her! He knew that she would be waiting for his call. She had told him that. Mel frowned. She didn't like the way all of this was making her feel. Neither one of them had much sleep the night before, and he also knew that she might be tired and want to get into bed early. So *where* the hell was he and *what* was he doing?

She glanced over at her phone, willing it to ring. Then suddenly she thought to dial his home number. *But what if he wasn't home?* she thought with irritation. No, she had too much pride to chase after him or to check up on him. He had said that he would call, and she would wait until he did so, she firmly decided.

She set the book down on the stand, picked up her sherry, downed the rest of it, and headed for her bedroom. She had to put him out of her thoughts so she could get some sleep. Apparently something had happened, she reasoned. Just because he didn't call tonight, it wasn't the end of the world. Things happen, she justified. Theirs was a new relationship, and she should give him the benefit of the doubt. She'd hear from him tomorrow, she thought. Then a really terrible thought popped into her head—what if something had happened to him? And what troubled her even more was that she had been doubting him, and had never for one minute thought that something or someone could have prevented him from getting to a phone. Boy, would she feel bad on two counts if something had gone wrong with him. Was she so insecure that she had to think that he had lied to her, or that he might even be out with someone else tonight? Or maybe she just didn't want to think that something could have happened to him, she suddenly thought. She felt better with that explanation.

Sitting down on her bed, she began to unbutton her blouse. The memory of their making love swept through her, and she immediately shuddered. She loved him, and was sure that he cared about her, and if she didn't hear from him by tomorrow, she would call him to make sure he was okay. With that resolved, she lay back. The minute her head touched her pillow, a faint scent of lime filled her senses, and his face and sunny smile appeared in her mind. He told her he'd be back soon, and she couldn't wait to be in his arms again to have him excite her as no man had ever done. They belonged together, they fit together, and as Helen said, it would work out.

Jim had returned to Fort Lauderdale feeling on top of the world. Melanie was everything he wanted in a woman and more. She was incredibly sexy and had satisfied him beyond belief. He couldn't wait to be with her and to wake up with her every morning wrapped in her arms.

Preparations for his relocation swirled through his mind. He had to get in touch with a real-estate agent to have his house put on the market, talk to movers, and see his boss, also his friend, about his leaving. He had already put him on notice about quitting, and he now had only the formalities to wrap up.

He stopped at his home to drop off his suitcase and to take care of some bills and phone calls that he'd put off. The minute he got home, he thought of calling Mel, but he knew how little sleep they had got, and, thinking she might have gone back to bed, didn't want to wake her. He decided that it would be better to reach her later in the day.

Just then his phone rang, and Jim dropped his suitcase, walked over to the telephone, and picked up the receiver.

"Hello," he stated cheerfully, suddenly hoping that it was Melanie.

"Jim, this is Ed. I'm glad that I caught you in."

Jim didn't fail to miss the anxiety in his boss's voice. "What's the trouble, Ed?" Jim immediately asked.

"Mark's out sick, and I can't reach anyone to fill in for him," he said with a harassed tone to his voice.

Jim was no dummy, he knew exactly what the implication of his boss's phone call was. "What time is the cruise?" Jim asked.

"The ship is scheduled to leave port at one," he retorted.

Jim glanced at his watch. Eleven o'clock. "That's not going to give me much time," he said.

"I know, but if you'll help me out, I'll give you a longer stretch of time off," his boss offered.

"Well, we'll have to talk about my changing jobs,

139

Ed. I've decided to go ahead and start my own business."

"I'm sorry to hear that, but I'll get busy on finding someone to replace you. So, what's your decision? Are you going to be able to go out today?"

"Yes, Ed, I'll be there as soon as I can."

"Thanks, Jim," Ed returned in a lighter tone.

"Sure," he returned, and then the line went dead.

As soon as he pushed the button down and got a dial tone, Jim called Melanie. To his chagrin, her line was busy. Cradling the receiver, he lifted his suitcase and walked toward his bedroom. Placing the case on his bed, he opened it and took out his rumpled clothes. Then he went over to his closet and began to pack.

When Jim was ready to leave for work, he tried Mel's number again, but it was still busy. Slamming down the receiver he headed for his car.

Before he got on board, he stopped in at his boss's office to pick up all the pertinent information related to the cruise. Spying one of Ed's secretaries, he approached the woman. Since he didn't know the new employee's name, he said, "Excuse me, but I have a favor to ask."

Looking up from her typewriter, she had a slightly annoyed look on her face.

"I'm sorry, I hope I didn't cause you to make a mistake," he stated, and flashed her his charming smile for good measure.

The woman's expression brightened. "It's difficult being new," she stated in an apologetic tone. "What did you want?"

Jim's smile broadened as he reached into his breast pocket and took out a folded piece of paper.

Handing it to the woman, he said, "This is my girl-friend's name and phone number, and I would like you to call her. I'm filling in for Mark as the captain of the next ship out of here, and I haven't been able to reach her to let her know."

The secretary smiled pleasantly and took the offered paper. She immediately opened it and looked over the number. Touching her glasses, she said, "I'll be happy to call her."

"Thanks, and what's your favorite perfume?" he asked with a wink.

Smiling, she shook her head. "Oh, you don't have to do that for me."

"What's the name?" He insisted.

" 'Le Dot'," she returned without further hesitation.

" 'Le Dot' it is, and thanks," he said.

The brunette immediately nodded in return, picked up the receiver, and began to dial.

"Oh, please finish your typing first. I just called her a few minutes ago, and her line was busy. Just try to reach her before you leave today, okay?"

"Yes, I will, and you are Mr. O'Dowd, aren't you?"

He laughed and answered, "Oh, right, details. I'm Jim O'Dowd. And your name?"

"Mary."

"I'm glad we got that settled. I could just imagine your getting Melanie on the line, and then not know-ing whom you were making the phone call for."

"Yes, that could have been a problem," she admit-ted with a laugh.

"Thanks again," he said, and started to walk away, but stopped. "And, Mary, give her my love and tell her that I'll be back in about five days," he added as he started to walk.

"I will. Good-bye, Mr. O'Dowd," she called after him.

Jim was really quite pleased about this last-minute cruise, because the upshot of it was that he could probably negotiate an earlier quitting date with Ed.

As he passed a phone, he decided to make one last attempt to reach her. He wanted to be the one who told her about the trip, and he also wanted to tell Melanie that he loved her. He dialed her number and waited as the phone rang. After the sixth ring, he gave up. No one could say that he hadn't tried, he thought with a shrug. He glanced at his watch and took off.

Just recently wed, Mary was a pushover for lovers. She couldn't help but think what a nice person this Jim O'Dowd was, and how lucky his girlfriend was.

She glanced down at her work and wondered how she was ever going to finish typing the stack of letters by the end of the day. She hadn't been exactly honest to her prospective employer about her typing speed, because she needed the job and seriously believed that she'd improve quickly with time. Suddenly feeling very pressured, she slipped Mr. O'Dowd's piece of paper under the corner of her typewriter, planning to call his friend at the end of the day, and began to type.

The following day was Saturday, and it crept by at a snail's pace, as Mel still hadn't heard from Jim. The rain did nothing to improve her mood, and instead of being occupied with projects to be done in her home, she felt encased in a tomb. Intuitively she couldn't believe that something had happened to him, and this thought made it more difficult for her to pick up the phone. So that meant he had lied to her. Anger began to build inside her, and with it her stubbornness.

Finally, by early evening she knew that she had to find out, once and for all, what had happened. She would never forgive herself if Jim were ill, and the knot in the pit of her stomach made her take some action. She immediately dialed his number, and her heart constricted as she waited for him to answer. But to her frustration, she received no immediate relief as the sound of the ring echoed through her brain.

Her irritation was mounting. Where was he? she wondered. If he *was* all right, then the man didn't have any excuse for not calling. She had to do something to shake off the way she was feeling. Then she suddenly thought that perhaps a long drive would help ease her tension as she grabbed her keys and yellow slicker. Driving always relaxed her, and she needed it to work some of its magic today.

Mel felt like a zombie as she walked stiffly toward the bathroom. She had tossed and turned the entire night, thinking about Jim. He still hadn't reached her, and she doubted for some reason that he would. She had called him far into the wee hours of the morning, and had not reached him. So, either he was in the hospital, or in another woman's arms, neither of which sat very well with her.

She glanced at her reflection in her mirror and couldn't believe how puffy her eyes were. She looked like a wreck! So much for falling in love, she thought with disdain. Her imagination was running wild, and she had to put a stop to it, because she never would have any answers until she talked to him. Helen came instantly to mind, and Mel automatically frowned, not wanting to dump her problems on her friend. Mel had hoped that she could handle her emotions with Jim, and it distressed her that she had allowed herself to get so quickly involved with this man and was now in so much pain because of it. She was embarrassed to admit this to Helen, not that her friend would be unkind, but because she had known better and had listened to her heart, instead of her head.

Splashing cold water on her face, Mel knew that she needed to talk to Helen, regardless of any trepidations that she might have. She had never in her life felt so angry and yet so helpless at the same time. For a normally happy, positive person these feelings were a bitter pill for Mel to swallow, as her whole life seemed in jeopardy of becoming unraveled. She didn't want to think the worst of Jim, and perhaps Helen could give her some reason for his behavior. With this resolved, she immediately turned to reach her friend.

Mel felt a little better now that Helen was coming right over to see her, quickly straightened up, and put on a pot of coffee.

As Helen's dark eyes peered over her cup at Mel, Mel admitted, "I can't believe what a fool I was. Just because I wasn't easy on the cruise, he had to hunt me down to prove his virility."

"Listen, we don't know that's the case. Maybe he just had an emergency and couldn't call," Helen suggested.

"I would have accepted that if today was Friday,

but this is Sunday, and what emergency could he have had?"

"Are his parents still living?"

"You know, I really don't know. There are so many things about him that I never learned. It's just that we never had the time to get to know each other better. We don't have the history together, so that I would know what to expect of him," Mel said in a discouraged voice.

"Have you tried to reach him?"

"Yes, I called all day yesterday and into the morning. Then I tried him again the minute I got up, but there was no answer."

Helen sighed. "Well, I still believe that he cares about you, Mel, so please try not to jump to any conclusions until you've talked to him. There really may be a good explanation why he hasn't called."

"Yes, I know, but it's so difficult not to think the worst."

"I just hope he's not in a jam."

"I know, Helen, I've thought of that, too, but I don't get the feeling that anything's happened to him," Mel uttered.

"Funny, I don't either," Helen remarked.

"So what should I do?"

"Have you tried his office?" Helen inquired.

Mel shook her head. "No, I didn't start calling him at home until yesterday."

"Then I'd say give him the benefit of the doubt and call him first thing tomorrow," Helen answered.

"And what if he's there?"

"Confront the bastard!" Helen asserted, and laughed. "Sorry, Mel, I couldn't resist that one."

"That's okay; frankly, that was my sentiment!" Mel retorted with a laugh.

Suddenly she realized that it had seemed like forever since she had laughed, and the sound was like a godsend. "Thanks, I needed that," Mel finally said.

"It'll work out," Helen reassured her.

"You keep saying that."

"Yes, and I really believe it," Helen insisted.

"Well, that makes me feel better," Mel admitted.

"You'll see."

"I hope so," Mel stated.

The women continued their discussion of Jim, then talked about the article, and finally made plans to get together at the end of the week to see a movie.

The night passed quickly, and Mel felt more optimistic about her captain.

But early the next morning, her fears returned as she dialed his office number.

A young woman's voice answered, "Hello, Marshall Cruises."

"Hello, I'd like to speak to Jim O'Dowd, please," she announced, and her chest tightened as she waited for the woman to speak.

"I'm sorry, but Mr. O'Dowd isn't in at the moment."

"Do you expect him soon?" Mel immediately inquired, as her need to have her anxiety resolved instantly outweighed the news that he was apparently all right.

"No, he's on a cruise right now, and we don't expect him back until around Friday. Is there anyone else who can help you?" the receptionist asked politely, while Mel's legs were buckling beneath her.

Tears welled up in her eyes as she answered, "No, there isn't."

"Would you like to leave a message?"

"No, it isn't important, but thanks just the same," Mel barely uttered, feeling as though her heart had just been shattered into a million pieces, and she slid down into the chair.

Moments passed while she stared blankly out into space as her world crumbled around her. It didn't make sense that he would have left on a cruise without telling her unless it *was* true that he really didn't care, that he had only pursued her to satisfy his male ego, and had lied about his being in her area to lure her into a false sense of security and into his clutches.

Suddenly the pre-recorded words "If you'd like to make a call, please hang up and try again; If you need assistance hang up and then dial your operator; Thank you" jolted her out of her thoughts. She glanced down in the direction of the sound and found her telephone receiver lying in her lap. Impatient that he was capable of causing her such disorientation and pain, she leapt up and slammed the receiver down on its hook.

"How dare he!" she fumed, getting angrier by the minute.

The sneak didn't even have the nerve to stick around to let her confront him. So the bastard was also a coward too! she thought with disgust. Pacing, she planned his demise as she mentally went over all the possible ways to get even, and finally decided that the one that afforded him the slowest death, where she could watch him squirm, would be her first choice.

Her favorites were the Chinese water torture, the Indian trick of burying a person's body up to his neck in sand and turning the ants on him, and then the much-written-about pit and pendulum. But it bugged Mel, because in order to choose the worst form of torture, she would have to know her victim's deep, dark fears, and, as she had recently discovered, she knew all too little about the deceitful captain.

Her thought of revenge was the only thing that stood between her and insanity, because she had never experienced such depth of rage, and seriously questioned whether she wasn't coming unglued. But there were only just so many ways that she could think of to do the man in, and only just so long that her anger could camouflage her pain before her body dissolved into racking sobs.

He was gone, out of her life, and it was as if the sunshine had been ripped from her heart and all laughter had stopped. She had thought of Jim as the perfect man, the kind that a woman dreamed about but rarely found. If it weren't so painful, perhaps she could find the humor in her mistake, but there had always been an element of unreality about their relationship, she reasoned, as she did a mental replay of their time together. It was just too good to be true, she decided, as she vowed to forget about Jim and concentrate on what she did have. The article came abruptly to mind, and Mel immediately identified with the victims she was writing about. This thought drove the nail into the coffin, and she seriously doubted whether she should be the one to write the story, feeling that she had lost her objectivity. But she decided to wait until tomorrow to see how she felt before talking to Helen.

Somehow, sometime, Mel fell miraculously into a deep sleep.

The sound of the phone ringing woke Mel, and it took her a few minutes before she made her way into the living room. Whoever it was, he was certainly persistent, she thought as the noise began to irritate her. To her surprise it was Helen.

"I couldn't wait to tell you—my editor in chief approved the article, loves the idea!"

"He does?"

"Yes, and I want to talk about—"

"I'm sorry for interrupting, but I have to talk to you about something, Helen. I've really thought about this a lot last night, and I don't think I should be the one to write it."

"You can't be serious."

"Yes, I am. I don't think that I'm objective enough."

"What happened, Mel?" Helen asked with sudden concern.

"I called Jim's office, and I was informed that he's on a cruise. He was supposed to be off this month, he told me that he was, and he never even called to let me know. You figure that out."

The line was dead for a moment before Helen said, "I don't know what to think now. But I do know that you should do the article, regardless of the captain. I'm very happy with the work that you've given me, and I know you'll do a good job. But if you don't want to write the article, then that's something else."

"Oh, of course, I want to write it, that's not the problem."

"Then get going on it, and we'll talk about what's-his-face later."

"You mean Jim?" Mel asked with a laugh.

"Yes, and don't worry, Mel, it'll be okay. I have another call waiting, and I'll phone you later."

"Fine. And, Helen, I'm really excited about the article, thank you for letting me know."

"You're most certainly welcome. Take care."

As their conversation ended, Mel suddenly felt rejuvenated. Helen's call was the best possible news she could have gotten. She now had a purpose, and it would help her keep in perspective that tall drink of water on the ocean where he belonged. She would get over the man; besides, they only had a few days together, it wasn't as if she'd spent years with him. At least she had found out about him now. It would have been much more painful to have discovered the truth about him months later.

She immediately thought about doing some writing and wondered if she shouldn't call the friends whom she'd first talked to about the cruise and get some of their experiences down on paper. She glanced at her clock and decided that Beth, also a teacher, would more than likely be at home, and Mel reached for her address book to look up her number.

The minute Jim left the ship, he called Melanie, but to his disappointment there was no answer. He had thought about getting a message through to her on several occasions, but there were so many problems on board that he wanted to wait until he could talk to her in person. He missed her terribly and was very anxious to see her again. He stood by the phone booth for a minute trying to decide if he should call her again. He really didn't feel like going home, because he wanted to see Melanie instead. Then it hit him—he'd just go out to the airport and take the first plane he could get to Pittsburgh. What a good idea! he thought, very pleased with himself.

As soon as Jim reached Pittsburgh, he tried Melanie's number again.

"Hello," she answered.

The instant he heard her silky voice, Jim smiled. "Hello there, yourself," he said happily. "I'm in town and I want to see you!"

To his surprise there was a click, and the line went dead. Annoyed that he'd been disconnected, Jim quickly redialed her number.

The minute he heard her say, "Hello," he said, "We were disconnected."

"What makes you think that?" she retorted, and the sound of the receiver being slammed down on its hook was heard.

Jim stared at the phone in disbelief. She had hung up on him! Was the woman crazy? Why in hell had she treated him that way? he wondered, totally baffled.

Well, he certainly was going to find out, he decided. If nothing else, she owed him an apology and that he would get, he thought determinedly as he rushed toward the car rental agency.

Mel was shaking. How dare he call her again and think that she'd be happy to hear from him after what he had pulled? The man had some nerve, she thought angrily. He must think that she was a complete idiot, a pushover, and desperate for him. Well, he had another think coming if he thought that he could just come sashaying back into her life after the stunt he had pulled, she fumed. The man just didn't know when he was well off, because if he darkened her door, she'd tell him a thing or two.

Then it suddenly occurred to her that he might just really try to see her, and that she'd better be prepared. So, she quickly changed into more flattering clothes—she wanted him to see what he'd lost—and then sat down in her father's leather chair to rehearse what she should say to him, because she wanted to make certain that she didn't leave anything out.

A few minutes later, there was a loud rap at her door at the precise time that it would take a speedy driver to get from the airport. She immediately jumped to her feet, feeling that she'd take care of him in a hurry.

The minute she saw the angry look in his eyes, she was startled, but quickly pulled herself together. "You wouldn't just happen to be in town for another business deal, would you?" she asked sarcastically.

"Why yes, I am. As a matter of fact, I hope to see Charlie to work out the last stages of our partnership," he stated, slightly taken aback by her tone of voice.

"So, you thought you could just drop by and I would be available," she retorted coolly, peering at him from behind the screen door, refusing to ask him in.

"I came to see you," he explained, seemingly surprised at her words.

"Well, I don't want to see you," she stated.

"Melanie, *what* the hell is going on here?" he asked loudly.

"Lower your voice, you're in my neighborhood," she warned.

"You owe me some kind of explanation," he demanded.

Mel hesitated a moment, thinking over what she was about to say. Steeling herself, she looked directly into his narrowed eyes. She'd had days to think about how badly he had treated her and how she would have liked to tell him off. But staring at him now, seeing the arrogance in him and the lack of remorse at what he'd done, she suddenly only wanted to lash out and hurt him the way he had hurt her.

"Simply put, you're not my type, and I don't want to see you," she said cruelly.

His features contorted with shock and anger. "You don't want to see me."

She swallowed hard, trying not to show any emotion in her voice. "Yes, that's correct," she replied.

"No, explanation, that's it?"

"That's right."

"You're some piece of work!" he retorted with contempt in his voice.

"Please leave," she ordered.

He stood there, tall and belligerent, his blue eyes darkened like angry thunderclouds, and then he turned to leave. Suddenly he pivoted sharply around, his eyes blazing. "I hope to God you know what you're doing!"

But he hadn't waited for any reply as he left in a huff.

Mel was trembling and moved quickly away from the door. She hadn't meant to be so cruel, but her own peace of mind was at stake, and she had to make sure that he wouldn't come back into her life to tear it apart again.

A numbness encased her, jarring her natural response to losing the man she loved. But she instinctively knew that it would be only a matter of minutes before the pain broke through, unleashing all the anguish and heartache that a person could ever endure.

Jim slipped into the car, slammed the door closed, and banged his hands against the steering wheel. *Women!* he fumed. How could she have treated him that way? Could he have been that far off in his judgment of her? He thought Melanie cared about him, the way that he cared about her, and he was thinking about marriage. Maybe something good came out of all this after all, he thought sarcastically—he'd been saved from marrying a schizoid person!

But nothing made sense to him. She really acted as though he had done something to her. But what could it be? he wondered. He recalled their last time together. She was fine when he left her, he told her that he would call her when he reached Florida, and she said that she was looking forward to hearing from him. Nothing strange there, he thought. Then he went to Fort Lauderdale, tried to call her, but she wasn't home, and he asked a secretary to call her. Perhaps something happened when Mary talked to Melanie. Immediately he inserted the key and started the ignition. He had to get to a phone and find out if he was right.

The minute he reached Mary, and she recognized his voice, the worry in her voice told him that something had happened.

"Oh, Mr. O'Dowd, I'm so glad you called," she exclaimed. "I know that you're going to be upset with me, and I'm sorry, but that day was so hectic that I misplaced her name and number."

"So you never reached her?" he asked in a deadly quiet tone.

"That's correct, and I am sorry. I remembered the 412 area code, but I couldn't recall her name to look up her number. I hope I didn't create any problems," she said regretfully.

Jim chuckled—a sardonic sound. More than he'd care to enumerate, he thought.

"Well, mistakes do happen, and I should have called her myself, or at least tried to get a message to her when I was aboard ship. So, don't worry any more about it."

He quickly ended their conversation, his mind already on Melanie and what she must have thought about not hearing from him. She probably had decided that he was only giving her a line to seduce her. He couldn't really blame her for being upset with him. After all, they hardly knew each other and lived apart, so it was conceivable that his actions could be misunderstood. But what bothered him the most was that she didn't even believe in him enough to think that perhaps there might be some kind of explanation.

Jim wondered what he ought to do. The end result was that he cared too much for Melanie to walk away. He knew he had to see her to explain what had happened; she'd have to decide then and there that she either trusted him or she didn't. Now the ball was in her court, it was all up to her.

As her anger wore off and the pain settled in, Mel wished that she had at least confronted him and given Jim the opportunity to explain why he hadn't called. Because she loved him, she still didn't want to think the worst of him and tried hopelessly to come up with a justification for his behavior. Besides, he had shown up at her home and truly seemed surprised and hurt by her reaction to him. A guilty man would have been prepared for her attack, which Jim obviously wasn't, she thought, her heart softening.

But instantly she was furious with herself for making excuses for the louse. How often had she heard that the murderer always returned to the scene of his crime to get some sadistic kick out of what he'd done? And to witness the effect of his deed upon other people? And perhaps the captain was even slicker than she had given him credit for, was better prepared than most liars, and had his "surprised and hurt" scenario rehearsed during his drive from the airport.

Mel's head was spinning. So many questions without answers nagged at her state of well-being and a nauseous feeling rose in the pit of her stomach. She didn't know what to think anymore and didn't even have the energy to try to figure it out.

Suddenly she heard a knock at her door. She instantly wondered who would be visiting her at this hour and wished that whoever it was would go away. But there was another knock, and Mel grudgingly pulled herself up, questioning who the hell it was, as she made her way to the door. One person she was sure it couldn't be was Jim.

As she glared through the screen door, her heart pounded against her chest and her breath caught in her lungs. There, standing in front of her, big as life, was Jim.

"You didn't think you'd get rid of me that easily," he snapped, his eyes filled with a challenging expression.

Seeing him made her want to laugh with joy, but his fierce look flashed her a warning.

"I didn't expect you, if that's what you mean?" she inquired coolly, not wanting him to know how happy she was to see him. He still had some questions to answer, she reminded herself.

"I should take you over my knee," he retorted.

She looked at him cross-eyed and piped, "I hope you brought someone to help you!"

He chuckled. "Boy, you're even more stubborn than I thought."

"Look who's calling the kettle black!"

"Hey, I wasn't the one who was nasty!"

Meeting his accusing eyes without flinching, she came back with "And I wasn't the one who didn't admit that he was a liar."

The words had just popped out, and she wished that she'd bitten her tongue. By his hostile glare, she knew that she was treading on thin ice.

"Are you going to make me stand out here all night? Or are you going to let me in and go somewhere with me to discuss this?" he inquired coldly.

She almost asked if they had something to discuss, but she was afraid to push her luck.

"Yes, I agree, I think we should talk," she admitted in a more friendly tone.

"Good. Well, what's it going to be? Here, or would you like to have a drink?" he asked in a voice that registered about the same degrees on the thermometer as his previous tone.

She could see that once he was fired up he was a hard nut to crack and wondered what she was about to hear. Taking a deep breath, she replied, "I think I need a drink," and silently thought that a restaurant would be a safer place in case their discussion got out of hand.

"A drink it is. I'll be waiting for you in the car," he announced, and walked briskly away.

Mel quickly checked her makeup and got a sweater before joining him.

Taking a gulp of his Scotch and soda, Jim stated, "I think I know why you are so upset with me."

"You do?" she asked with ruffled brow.

"Yes, and I'm disappointed that you didn't care enough to ask me what had happened."

"Something happened?"

"No, I mean, yes," he retorted irritably. "You were angry because I didn't call and thought I didn't care, right?"

"Yes, on both counts."

He sighed and nodded. "That's what I figured happened," he said in a weary tone.

Mel stared at him in disbelief. The guy might have everything worked out in his head, but he was forgetting one very important thing—he hadn't explained anything to her.

"So what's the story?" she asked impatiently.

His eyes suddenly focused as though he had been lost in thought. "Oh, I'm sorry, Melanie, I was just thinking how preposterous this all was. You really want to know what happened?"

"Yes, of course, I do," she said with irritation in her voice. What'd he think she was sitting there for—her health?

"When I got back, I learned that one of the captains was out with the virus, and my boss caught me at home the minute I walked in the door, wanting me to fill in for the guy. I knew that he would tend to be a little bit more understanding about my quitting earlier than we'd discussed if I did him the favor. So I agreed to go out on the cruise the same day, and I tried to call you a few times, but your line was busy. I had only two hours to get my shipping papers and to get ready. Then there was this new secretary, Mary, to whom I gave your name and number and asked her to call you. I even tried to reach you again before I boarded ship, but then there wasn't any answer. And I just assumed that Mary had called you. When I got back into port, I had to see you and took the first plane I could get."

Mel reflected about her line being busy and realized that he could be telling the truth, but when he called her from the airport, he hadn't said anything about this Mary trying to reach her then, nor had he mentioned her when he arrived at her home. Had he only invented the woman when he realized that Mel wasn't the same easy woman whom he had left?

Mel sipped her wine and asked suspiciously, "How did you know that Mary didn't call me?"

"Well, I'm no dummy. I went over everything in my

mind. It didn't make sense to me that you were so angry at me unless of course you were a crazy person. Then it came to me that maybe you never got Mary's phone call, so I called the office and spoke to her."

"You did?"

"Yes, and she told me that she had so much work that day that she somehow happened to misplace the piece of paper that I gave her."

Mel leaned back in her chair, thinking his words made sense. "I couldn't imagine what had happened to you. I even thought you might have been in an accident, and I was out of my mind with worry," she admitted.

"I'm sorry I put you through all that. I should have tried to get a message to you, but everything was such a mess on the ship that I was too hassled to think straight."

"Well, I'm glad you're all right now," she said.

"Aren't you happy to see me?"

"Yes, I am but I didn't know what to think. You said that you'd call me as soon as you got back, and when I didn't hear from you by Saturday, I thought that something happened at the airport or you were ill. I really didn't want to think the worst of you."

"I feel better about that," he exclaimed.

"Then I called your office on Monday and found out that you were on a cruise—that did it for me."

"You called? I never got any message."

"I never left one," she replied.

"I really care about you, Melanie, and I was disappointed that you didn't think that there might have been some kind of mix-up."

"I suppose I did jump the gun a little, and I have to

160

admit that I was influenced by what I heard about ship's officers' reputations and what I saw on the cruise. I should have given you the benefit of the doubt, and at times I did, but I just couldn't find an explanation for your not calling."

"You did mistrust me a lot, didn't you?"

"Yes. I didn't know you well enough, and I had only my feelings to go on. And sometimes everything got so muddled, I didn't know what was happening. I only knew how attractive you were, and I was afraid that I was listening to my heart and not to my head."

Jim shook his head. "Now everything makes sense.

"I don't understand, Jim."

"I always had the feeling that I was with two people when I was with you. At times you seemed so open, and other times so protective. Your behavior confused me and put me on guard."

Mel laughed. "Boy, it's a wonder that we ever got together."

Jim chuckled in return. "You've got a point there."

Mel raised her glass in salute. "To no more misunderstandings and to communication."

"I'll second that," Jim came back and tapped her glass with his.

A silence suddenly came over them as they both drank their cocktails. Mel couldn't believe how much better she felt. She felt as though she were going to live again, as a warm glow settled over her.

CHAPTER EIGHT

"Would you like to have dinner?" Jim asked.

She looked over at his handsome face and replied, "Why not?"

"I was hoping that maybe we could go back to my hotel to fool around a little first," he said seductively.

She wanted to be in his arms, there was no doubt about that, but she did wonder if she shouldn't wait. He had said nothing about his plans and, even though what he told her made sense, she still wasn't entirely over her pain.

"What's the matter, Melanie? We don't have to go if you don't want to. I've missed you so much and I wanted to hold you, that's all," he murmured, his eyes earnestly fixed on her.

"I've missed you too, Jim."

"Forget that I said anything. Where would you like to go for dinner, or would you like to stay here?"

"I don't know."

Suddenly she wasn't very hungry, and the thought of being alone with him instantly excited her.

"I would like to change," she admitted, glancing down at her trousers.

"I'll take you home, then," he said.

"Okay," she replied, and could have sworn that her cheeks had grown warm.

She hadn't fooled anyone. Her worldly captain probably knew that she wanted to be in his arms more than anything. And again, she had given him two different signals.

They quickly finished their drinks, and Jim took her home.

Once inside, Mel held out her arms to him, and he immediately enfolded her in his. Her heart rejoiced as she felt his body come alive next to hers. He bent over and brushed his lips vehemently against hers. Abruptly he broke away and stared down at her.

"Please don't ever doubt me again. I was so afraid that I had lost you," he exclaimed. "Hold me!"

She wrapped her arms tightly around him and cried, "Darling, it's been so long!"

In answer to her unspoken prayer, with trembling hands, he began to undress her.

A few hours later, after dinner at one of Melanie's favorite spots, she sat across from Jim, smiling. She knew that anyone who looked at her could see the rosy glow of their lovemaking on her face. But she didn't care. She wanted the world to see how much she loved this man, this adorable redhead with her.

"You're so beautiful," he remarked fondly.

"I feel beautiful, thanks to you," she came back playfully.

"You give me too much credit, Melanie. You're such a warm and giving person, and I feel so lucky that I've found you."

"Thank you, Jim," she whispered.

"It's true, or I wouldn't say it. You don't really know me, but I can be pretty blunt sometimes," he admitted.

"Not you!" she teased.

He laughed. "I guess I left myself open for that one."

"And I never miss an opportunity," she stated in a cocky tone.

"I've noticed that. You were really rough on me earlier."

Mel glanced down at her coffee cup and frowned, annoyed that he had to bring that up.

"I said I was sorry," she replied.

His eyebrows were raised in disbelief.

"If I didn't, I meant to," she stated, slightly miffed.

"Boy, you take the cake," he said with a chuckle.

"Okay, so I hate admitting that I made a mistake," she said with slight irritation.

"Did anyone ever tell you that you were cute?"

"No, you were the first," she lied with a grin.

He shook his head. "There's never going to be a dull moment in this relationship."

Mel laughed, glancing around the room. Suddenly her eyes caught sight of two of her girlfriends, and one of them was looking directly at her. It was Beth, to whom she had just talked to about the article, and Beth was not the most discreet person in the world; she had a tendency to talk before she thought, even though she was always apologetic afterward.

To her mortification, Beth was walking toward their table with an eager look in her eye, and Mel immediately expected the worst. Mel realized that she had automatically braced herself against the table and her nails were digging into the wood.

Out of the corner of her eye, she saw Jim staring at her strangely, and turning to him, forced a smile.

"Are you all right? You're as white as a ghost?" Jim asked.

Mel laughed hysterically. "Remember me in the sheet?"

"Yes," he answered, not in the least bit amused.

Then thinking the best bet was to get out of the restaurant before Beth blew her cover, she said, "I'm stuffed. What do you say we go to my place to relax?"

"Now you're talking," he said, a little more responsive.

He immediately glanced around the room, looking for their waiter.

Mel held her breath and hoped that she could leave before anything was said. She knew that she had to tell him about the article, but it would be awkward if he heard about it from someone else. He'd probably never forgive her, and she wouldn't blame him. But all her fast thinking was wasted, for the perky blonde had reached their table and immediately exclaimed, "Why, Mel, I didn't expect you here. I thought you said you were going to be working on that article of yours."

"I was, but my friend here came in from out of town," she answered curtly.

"I'm Beth, what's your name?" she asked, extending her hand to Jim.

"Jim," he answered, and quickly shook her hand.

"Did she tell you about the article she's writing? I can't wait to see it. She even used some of the experiences I had on one of my cruises."

"You don't say," Jim retorted with tight jaw.

Beth swung around to Mel and inquired cheerfully, "Well, how is your article on the wolf pack coming?"

By the darkened look in Mel's eyes and her delayed response, Beth finally realized her mistake. Glancing over at her friend, Beth said, "Oh, I see Jane is anxious to go. Nice meeting you, Jim, and, Mel, I'll talk to you later."

Her eyes had signaled their regret, and Mel automatically nodded to her. By the dark look in Jim's eyes, she knew that the damage had already been done, and Mel realized that she now had to concentrate upon finding the right words that would help him understand why she hadn't told him herself about the article.

"How very interesting," he remarked sarcastically.

"What's that?" she asked innocently.

"Do I have to spell it out for you?" he inquired in a nasty voice.

"No, you don't," she admitted, wondering how on earth she was going to get out of this one.

"So, tell me about this article," he persisted.

"Where shall I start?" she asked in a small voice.

"At the beginning. I have all night." He leaned back in his chair and folded his arms.

Mel suddenly preferred a firing squad to this man as he glared at her with burning, reproachful eyes.

"Okay," she said, and took a breath. "I was bored and wanted to do something different, something exciting."

"And you decided to go on a cruise," he interrupted impatiently.

She stared at him. If these were to be her last words, then she wanted to be the one who spoke them.

"Excuse me, but I am the one who is supposed to be giving this confession, and if you interrupt me, I may lose my train of thought," she asserted, not knowing where she had gotten such confidence.

"You're perfectly right; I certainly don't want you to leave anything out."

His tone had not been very pleasant, and Mel suddenly felt very warm around the neck. He wasn't going to make it easy on her, he was out for blood, *her* blood, and the quicker she got on with it the better.

"I was a little nervous about traveling alone. That's where Beth comes in. She is one of the women I knew who had gone on cruises. I was told that I should go, that being onboard a ship was a great experience, but I was also warned about the wolf pack."

Jim raised his eyebrows as if he were about to talk, but Mel held up her finger to warn him not to.

"Let me finish," she stated, then waited a moment before she continued. "I talked to Helen and told her about my wanting to go on a cruise and what I had heard. She suggested that I should go and that I should write about my experiences. She thought it would make an interesting article. And that's about it," she stated, clasping her hands together, feeling lucky that she was still alive to tell her story.

"So what's the *about* part?" he inquired with dead eyes.

"Well . . ."

"Go on, Melanie, we don't want to leave the best part out."

"I don't like your attitude," she came back.

"Why did Beth ask you how your article on the wolf pack was coming?" he inquired, ignoring her complaint.

Mel laughed nervously as she toyed with the napkin on her lap. "Well, the wolf pack, as you know, referred to the officers who seduced lonely women passengers."

"Please stop me if I'm wrong, but your article was about seduction," he stated sharply.

"Yes, I suppose you could say that," she admitted. "I was writing the article to show what happens aboard ship and how some women get taken advantage of."

"And what about the wolf pack? Don't you think that some of them are snared by these poor, helpless creatures?"

She suddenly wondered if he was referring to her snaring him, but she bit her tongue. She didn't want to get into any more arguments.

"Yes, I did meet some women who booked the cruise only to have a fling."

"To seduce the officers," he corrected.

"Yes, that's true."

"So, all the time we were together, you were keeping notes?"

"Jim, that's not exactly the way it was."

"That's precisely the way it was," he snapped.

"You've got it all wrong," she insisted, but she knew it was hopeless, her words were falling on deaf ears.

"When were you going to tell me about it? I might have been able to give you some good pointers," he added sarcastically.

"That's not fair!" she insisted.

"Am I in your article?"

"Well, yes," she admitted.

"And you want to talk about being fair! Everything now makes sense—the schizoid behavior, the talking into the tape recorder, and your dating me after you wouldn't even give me your phone number!"

"But, Jim, you've got it all wrong," she protested.

"No, I think you're the one who has it all wrong!" he fumed, and threw down his napkin as he stood.

"Don't do this, Jim!" she exclaimed.

"I loved you, and to you—I was only a guinea pig! an experiment!" he spat out, and started to leave.

Mel instantly wondered how she would pay the bill, because she hadn't brought any money with her.

"And don't worry, I'll take care of the check on my way out!" he snapped back, and took off.

If Mel had thought restaurants were safe places to avoid public outbursts, she just learned how wrong she had been. She could feel everyone's eyes on her and she had never felt so humiliated in her life! That's what came of her falling in love, she thought, and she'd have to remember not to do it again. Then like a bolt of lightning it hit her! He had said he loved her! But he also felt that she had merely used him, she reminded herself. The stupid idiot! she thought. Didn't he know how much she cared?

From the moment that she saw Beth, her defenses went up, numbing all her senses and putting her mind on automatic pilot. She had hardly heard him tell her that he loved her, and now that she had remembered, it was too late. Jim was gone.

Jim returned to Florida, totally disgusted with all women. Here all the time he had been worried about her trusting him! he thought sarcastically. Boy, he would like to get his hands on that article. Maybe he could sue her. Dragging her through court and letting the world see her underhanded ways would certainly make his day! What a fool he'd been, he fumed as he poured himself a drink.

Turning on the TV and flopping down onto his sofa, he wondered what he had done so wrong to deserve a woman like Melanie. She was bad news in the disguise of an innocent-looking schoolteacher, and had he been taken in! So much so that he had allowed himself to fall madly in love with the fallen angel. There was no justice in life, he thought as he glanced at the darkened screen. He looked at his watch and realized that the station had already gone off the air.

He jumped up, snapped the TV off, and walked over to the window, staring out into the pitch-black night.

Since knowing Melanie, his whole world had been turned upside down. Now he didn't even know if he wanted to start that partnership; perhaps being near Melanie was not a good idea. But then again, he didn't have to live in that area. Perhaps he could stay in Florida and work from there. He might have to make some trips to Pittsburgh, but his chances of running into her were unlikely. That made sense to Jim, and he felt a little better about working with Charlie. It really would have irritated the hell out of him knowing that Melanie had caused him to give up something he wanted to do.

Melanie. She certainly was an operator; his angel was in reality a spy. All the time he held her in his arms, he thought that she was truly reacting to him, but instead, she was probably excited that she had gotten some more information for her article. For a bright man, he couldn't believe how easily he had been duped by a pretty face. And for what—some stupid article! She must never have cared about him, because how could she risk losing him by continuing with the assignment? She ought to have realized that he would be upset. That made sense, he reasoned, but she went ahead with the article anyway, and used him as one of the wolves!

Women! If his experience with Melanie was typical, then he had to learn to live without them. In the meantime, when Monday morning came around, he would sign up for any cruises that were scheduled. This way he would have the time he needed to sort things out. Starting the partnership had looked more appealing when he felt that Melanie was going to be in his life, but now, since he knew better, he had to rethink his plans for the future.

Finally he thought he could sleep. It was all too much for a grown man to handle. But it was amazing what a difference a day made, he thought sadly, and then laughed at himself as he remembered those were the words to a song. But his sense of humor faded quickly as loneliness took hold of him. The feeling was so deep and so real that all he could compare the experience to was what he imagined a baby felt when he awakened in the night without his mother there.

He suddenly realized why he had fallen head over heels in love with Melanie. She had a way of grounding him, and making him feel important and secure. It was funny that one woman could do all that, but somehow, in between talking into her tape recorder, she had managed to work her wiles on him. He knew he would miss her, but he also came to the conclusion that they had nothing in common and that he would never contact her. He was going out to sea, he was putting as much distance between them as he could, and he was going to forget her. With that resolved, he walked toward his bedroom.

Mel managed to get her life back on a somewhat even keel. After Jim left, she began writing her article and resumed some of the friendships she'd had before she met Jim. But instead of distracting her, the men she saw only painfully reminded her of what she was missing as she compared them all to him. A day didn't go by without her thinking of him, as his name lingered around the edges of her mind.

Several times she picked up the receiver to call him, but then remembered the look of disgust in his eyes just before he left, and she was still too vulnerable to risk his rejection.

One evening Helen asked Mel to her home for dinner. Mel suspected that her friend was concerned about her and wanted to know what had happened with Jim.

"So why so quiet about what's-his-face?" Helen finally inquired.

"Because there's nothing to tell. It's all over," Mel responded sadly.

"And you didn't tell me!"

"There was nothing that could be done and I was in pain and thought I should be alone."

"Well, if I can help in any way, please let me know," Helen stated with concern.

"I don't know what to do," Mel said feebly.

"I can't help if I don't know the problem."

"He found out about the article," Mel admitted.

"So what's wrong with that? He should be proud about it," Helen insisted.

"Well, he knows that I wrote about him, and he thinks he's one of the wolf pack. I really didn't explain it very well," Mel stated.

"I see."

"And he got very angry, told me that he loved me, while I was treating him like a guinea pig, and stormed out of the restaurant."

"This happened in a restaurant?" Helen asked, wide-eyed.

"Yes, we were at Paradise Inn, and he played the gentleman right to the end and picked up the check on his way out."

"Well, you have to admit, that was nice of him."

"That's the point, Helen. I would have preferred that he'd done something rotten, that way I wouldn't feel so miserable."

"And you haven't heard from him since?"

"No, and by the way he looked at me, I don't expect to. But I've tried to call him, that is until the thought of his lashing out at me comes to mind, and then I hang up the receiver."

"Well, Mel, the two of you have to talk."

"I agree, but I know he doesn't want to talk to me."

"How do you really know that? The guy said that he loved you, and I think he meant it."

"You do?" Mel asked in a surprised tone.

"Certainly, or why else would he tell you that? If all he was after was sex, he had already gotten what he wanted. Why don't you call him?" Helen urged.

"What would I say?"

"You could start by telling him that you love him," Helen insisted.

"It's too late for that. He couldn't care less whether I lived or died," Mel said in a quiet voice.

"You don't know that."

"Oh, yes, I do. The night he walked out on me, he already had me dead and buried."

"Mel, how on earth are you ever going to patch this up if you don't try?"

"Helen, I will try to reach him, but I'm not ready yet. I'm afraid if I get him on the phone and he says something nasty, I'll burst into tears. I don't want to do that."

"Well, all right, but I wouldn't let too much time go by without reaching him, because when you do, he may just think that it's too late."

"That's the chance I have to take, isn't it?" Mel inquired stubbornly.

Helen's eyes darkened as she shook her head. "For two bright people you are certainly acting stupidly."

"What's that supposed to mean?"

"It's obvious, Mel, that you and Jim are really in love with each other, but you're both letting your pride stand in the way. Sure I can understand how hurt he might have been when he learned about the article, especially if he wanted you to be open with him."

"Yes, I did hurt him, but he never even gave me a chance to explain anything to him. He just huffed off into the night like some creature from the dark lagoon."

Helen studied her, giving her that serious look when she wasn't buying what Mel said.

"Oh, okay, what's up? Why are you looking at me that way?" Mel asked.

"I think we've got something else going on here."

"What's that?"

"I don't think you're being completely honest with yourself," Helen insisted.

"I still don't know what you're talking about."

"I've listened to what you said, especially the part about why you're not getting in touch with Jim, and I think what you haven't said is that you're scared."

Helen paused and waited for Mel to respond, but she didn't.

Then she continued, "I don't know why it is, but I think you're afraid of this relationship, and a part of you is gladly letting it go because you don't want to deal with it."

Mel thought over her friend's words and had to admit that there was some element of truth there. Right from the beginning, her reaction to Jim had bothered her more than anything Jim did or said to her.

"I suppose you're right. I've never experienced such intense feelings, and I pushed him away. It wasn't entirely me questioning his motives, but my emotions. But I'm not ready to get in touch with him, because—"

"You have to be certain that you really want him," Helen interrupted.

"I want him, but I'm . . ."

"Afraid?"

"Yes, Helen, I'm scared to death," Mel admitted as tears came into her eyes.

"It's perfectly understandable. This is a first for you, so be kind to yourself."

"Thanks, Helen, you're wonderful. I think you'd better put up a shingle stating that a shrink's available," she said, and laughed, glancing down at her watch.

Helen laughed too. "That sounds like what I always say to you!" The twinkle in Helen's eyes made Mel smile as she stood up.

"Thanks for the lovely dinner, it was really great," Mel said cheerfully.

"I'm glad you liked it," Helen said, and as Mel started toward the door, she gently patted Mel on the back and added, "Don't worry, everything will be all right."

Mel smiled her thanks before leaving.

As Helen began cleaning up the dinner dishes, she couldn't believe how upset Mel was. They had grown up together, and she had never seen her friend this hurt, and it tore at Helen's heart to see her friend in so much pain. She felt helpless and wished that there were something she could do for Mel. She racked her brain, but it wasn't until she began to wash the plates that an idea took shape. First, she had to get them together. So, she'd have to call Jim's office to find out where he was, and then she'd have to figure out a way to get the two lovebirds together. But she didn't have his office number, she immediately thought with a frown. Oh, yes, she did, she reminded herself, remembering that when she helped Mel plan her cruise, she had gotten his company's number. All she had to do was dial that number, and she would be referred to his office. Clever, she thought, pleased with herself.

Helen suddenly felt more optimistic about the two lovebirds, and knowing that it was too late to do anything about it now, she decided to call his company first thing in the morning.

CHAPTER NINE

Helen, true to her word, called Jim's office and found out that he was on a cruise. The instant she learned his schedule, she called Mel and told her the news.

"Mel, he couldn't call you even if he wanted to. The man's on the ocean."

"You mean he's out on another ship?"

"Yes, precisely."

"How did you find that out?"

"Well, I couldn't just sit by and watch you suffer, so I called his office and found out where he was," Helen admitted.

"You didn't?" Mel asked with surprise in her voice.

"I sure did. And I've been giving this situation of yours a lot of thought, and I think it's understandable that Jim was hurt hearing about the article from someone else. He obviously doesn't know how much you care about him, and I think you should catch up with his cruise when his ship anchors at Barbados."

"Are you serious?"

"Never been more serious in my life. What do you want to do, Mel, end up an old spinster, thinking about the man you let get away?"

Mel laughed. "As I've said many times before, you have a way of cutting the mustard."

"I don't think you've ever put it exactly that way before," Helen shot back with a laugh.

"You've certainly given me something to think about," Mel said with a sigh.

"Well, don't think too long, you've only got two days to reach him."

"He'll think I'm a fool," Mel exclaimed.

"He'll think you're a woman who knows what she wants and isn't afraid to go after it," Helen retorted.

"What will I say to him when I see him?"

"Tell him that you love him," Helen said simply.

"Where did you say he'd be?" Mel inquired with more enthusiasm in her voice.

"Barbados."

"Oh, Helen, I'm going to do it! What do I have to lose? Either he really loves me and wants to be with me, or he doesn't. But this way I'll know for sure," Mel said optimistically.

"Now, you're talking!"

"I've never done anything like this before," Mel exclaimed.

"It's about time," Helen stated.

"There's so many things to do," Mel said.

"I'll call my travel agent and get a list of flights available," Helen offered.

"Oh, thanks, Helen," Mel replied happily.

Mel stood on the Barbados dock, the heat of the sun beating down on her head and her heart in her throat, as she anxiously awaited to board ship. She resolved to find out, once and for all, where they stood. The day of reckoning couldn't be postponed, and she looked forward to seeing her captain again.

It seemed like hours when only minutes had passed as she grew restless, her body rigid and her eyes fixed on the ocean. She recalled the thrill of being held against Jim's strong body, the way his sweet mouth caressed hers, and every detail of his face. A shiver of vivid recollection spread through her, and she wondered whether he would be happy to see her. She hoped he would, but she didn't expect any miracles.

Finally Mel was taken aboard, shown to her cabin, and then left to her own devices. Once in her stateroom, she quickly unpacked and changed into the blue dress that Jim had complimented her on and seemed to like so much. She quickly curled her hair, redid her makeup, and sprayed on some perfume. Glancing at her image in the mirror on the way to the door, she stopped short. Her actions suddenly reminded her of a knight preparing himself for battle, instead of a woman getting ready to greet her lover. Mel had to laugh at her last-minute jitters. She loved Jim, and she knew that she would find a way to get through that pigheaded skull of his.

With nothing but positive thoughts, Mel took off in search of Jim. She carefully scanned all the uniformed men, but to her disappointment Jim was nowhere to be found. Her spirits were not daunted, as renewed energy charged her on. He was somewhere around, she could sense his presence, and it was only a matter of time until she found him. She would track him down even if she had to follow him to the end of the world, she pledged with steadfast determination. And if he wasn't happy to see her, then she'd let him have it with both barrels about his ungentlemanly act of walking out on her in the restaurant. She suddenly felt as if she were parading in a victory march as she almost heard "The Land of Hope and Glory" playing in the background as she scurried about.

But as she surveyed the ship, she found herself automatically slipping back into the past. She thought about the Harpers and wondered whether they were planning their next cruise. She could still picture the first time she saw Jim standing on the bridge, staring down at her with the most magnetic grin that she had ever seen. But suddenly, without warning, the memory of his ruggedly handsome face contorted with disgust just before he left her flashed before her mind's eye, and a sick feeling radiated through her stomach. Her steps faltered as her courage melted through the haze of doubts.

Instantly she decided that she needed some air, thought about going to the deck, and swung abruptly around. But unfortunately her way was blocked as she collided with what felt like a brick wall. Startled, her lashes fluttered. She was staring into a gold button at the top of a uniform and at a neck that looked familiar, and Mel tensed. Her glance crept slowly upward, as she braced herself for the worst.

Jim was glaring down at her! So many thoughts swirled through her head, but her first instinct was to throw herself into his arms. But as her vision cleared, his pale eyes were like bits of stone, chilling her to the bone and riveting her to the spot.

"You should watch where you're going," he stated as his hands held her arms.

Wriggling herself free from his clutches, she retorted, "Typical, *you* would say something like that!"

"You act as if I ran into you," he replied curtly.

Her eyes narrowed as she wondered how on earth she had ever found anything nice about this man.

"Aren't you even a little bit surprised to see me?" she asked as she automatically tapped her foot.

"Well, yes, but then I figured that with me gone, you ran out of material, and now you're on a spy mission for some more," he replied in a cocky tone.

"You think you've got it all figured out, don't you?"

"*You* I do," he retorted.

"You think so?" she asked with challenging eyes.

"Of course. Once you get to the core of a rotten apple, it's easy as pie."

"I came here, smart guy, to see you to tell you how much I cared about you, but you're too much of a stubborn idiot to see beyond your big nose!" she shot back, turning sharply on her heel, and sped away.

Well, if that's how it was, then she would play the cards that were dealt her! She couldn't jump ship, and there was plenty to occupy her, so she'd make the best of it. Quickly she made her way to the cocktail lounge to have a drink and to start her life anew.

She was on her second drink, feeling better by the minute, when somebody tapped her on the shoulder. Instantly thinking that the captain had had a change of heart, her spirits rose. But regardless of how pleased she was, she felt he deserved to squirm a bit.

Another, more insistent tap was felt, and Mel thought he must be getting a little anxious, and smiled to herself.

Feeling that she'd finally let him wiggle long

enough, she turned with a grin on her face and looked up.

Oh, good grief! she thought, and almost died, feeling as though someone had just pricked her balloon.

"Look who's here!" Tom West said as he smiled at her. "I guess you're going to become one of our regulars," he added in a knowing way.

She was about to tell him to shove off when suddenly over Mr. West's shoulder she spied Jim heading her way.

"What does it take to be a member of this special group?" she inquired sweetly, but secretly wished to punch him in the nose.

He gave her one of his cocky grins and replied arrogantly, "From the first moment I saw you, I thought you were the type of lady I'd like to get to know. What are you drinking?"

"An extra-dry martini on the rocks, please," she said, raising her empty glass.

His eyebrows rose in awe. "Boy, looks can be deceiving," he said with appreciation.

As Tom turned to order her drink, she smiled pleasantly and called out, "Why, hello there, Captain! Fancy meeting you here!"

"Don't you think you've had enough?" he inquired, the minute he reached her.

"I've only just begun," she retorted with challenging eyes. "Tom and I are celebrating. Would you like to join us?" she asked coyly.

"Mr. West has some duties to attend to, don't you, Mr. West?" he ordered more than asked.

Tom turned abruptly, caught the stern look in the captain's eyes, and replied, "Oh, yes, sir, I do, but I'll see you later, Miss Ford." He then slipped her a wink and disappeared.

"That was a rotten thing to do!" she snapped.

"Boy, out of the frying pan into the fire," he stated, shaking his head.

"We were having a good time, and you had to come along and spoil it," she said with annoyance.

"You really must be desperate for material," he stated with a frown.

"Why are you being so difficult, when with a little help, you'd be impossible?" she spat out.

As her martini was placed in front of her, she reached for it, but Jim took it away. Ignoring her, he ordered, "Bartender, I want to sign the check."

"I'm tired of your treating me like a child," she objected.

"Have you eaten?" he asked with concern.

"It's none of your business," she came back.

"I want to take you to dinner," he exclaimed.

"Well, I don't want to go," she answered stubbornly.

"Well, sometimes you don't know what's good for you," he stated as he turned to sign the check.

"Please leave me alone."

He looked back at her, the pen still held in the air, and exclaimed, "I don't want to leave you alone. Try that on for size."

"Jim, you had your chance, and you let me go."

"Just a minute," he stated, and glanced down at the bill.

"I don't have a minute," she replied, hopping off the bar stool and leaving.

She was tired of this nonsense. All of a sudden, now

184

he was acting so concerned about her well-being! Well, it was too late!

But she was no match for the speed of the captain as he caught up with her outside the lounge, grabbed her around the waist, and stated, "Mel, please don't go!"

"Let me go, someone might be looking!" she demanded angrily.

"I don't care if the world's watching, I am happy to see you."

"Let go of me," she repeated, trying to break his hold.

"Only if you promise not to take off again," he stated.

"You're a fine one to talk about taking off!" she snapped.

"Okay, I deserved that one," he admitted.

"You deserve a lot more than that. Now, let me go, this is ridiculous!" she ordered, pushing against his arms.

In spite of her struggling, he brought her tightly up against him. The instant she felt his body pressed against hers all her reserve melted away. The rotten guy would have to pull this trick on her, she silently fumed.

Mel sighed. "I won't take off. There, I said it. Now, get your big paws off me!"

Jim chuckled, which enraged her all the more, and he immediately released her.

She straightened her dress, and with as much dignity as she could muster, turned to face him. "Strong-arm tactics suit you well," she retorted.

"How about something to eat?" he asked, not bothered by her words in the least.

"Sounds like a good idea," she returned, but suddenly feeling a little tipsy, corrected, "I think I'd like some coffee."

"How about if we went to my stateroom and had some there?" he inquired.

She eyed him suspiciously.

"It's quiet, we can talk," he explained innocently.

"If you put it that way, okay," she agreed, assured that he intended no funny business.

Seated in a chair in his cabin, she watched him as he dialed room service and wondered what he wanted to talk about.

Cradling the receiver, he turned to her with a smile and said, "It should be here in a few minutes."

"So, what did you want to say?" she asked immediately, not wanting to be kept in suspense any longer.

"What are we going to do?" he asked with serious eyes.

"What are the options?" she inquired wearily.

"You said you cared about me, is that correct?"

"So, you did hear me," she said.

"Melanie, there's only so much guff I'm willing to take from you," he stated, slightly irritated.

"And then what?" she demanded, not liking his tone of voice.

She was the one who had chased after him, after he had dropped her like a hot potato, and he didn't even have the decency to apologize.

"I see this is getting us nowhere. What's wrong, Melanie?"

She stared at him, but refused to answer him.

"So, it's for you to know and me to find out. Is that what it is?" he asked with soft, pleading eyes.

She suddenly felt very foolish and didn't have the heart to continue on with this verbal tit for tat. She loved him, but out of stubbornness she hadn't wanted to back down.

She began slowly, "There's a lot wrong here, Jim. I think that's obvious."

"Yes, but I want to try to work things out with you. I've had enough time to think about what happened. I was very hurt and disappointed by you," he admitted.

"And now?"

"Now I'm just really happy to see you. I'm sorry that I didn't let you know that. But *why* didn't you tell me about the article, Melanie?"

"I wanted to, but I was afriad you'd get the wrong idea."

"I don't mean to put you on the defensive, but I don't think I'm getting the whole story."

Mel sighed and nodded her head. "I suppose you're right. You want the truth?"

"Shoot."

"Now, if you hear something you don't like, are you going to get up and go storming off?" she quizzed.

He gave her a downcast expression and exclaimed, "I'm sorry about that."

"Thank you," she returned in a quiet voice.

"Please go ahead, I'm here for the night," he stated with a boyish grin.

"What about your work?"

He glanced at his watch and replied, "I'm okay for a while."

"The truth of the matter, Jim, is that I fell for you too quickly, that I was unsure of my emotions, and I questioned yours. This is all very new for me, and I was terribly confused."

"What's new for you?"

"Being in love. It scares me beyond belief," she said, her voice drifting into a hushed whisper as tears came to her eyes.

"Darling," he exclaimed, and made a move toward her.

She raised her hand. "No, please let me finish. At times, I really did believe that you were like the manipulative womanizers that I was writing about," she admitted as her thin fingers twisted in her lap.

His soft expression hardened.

"I told you, you might not like what I said," she stated. "When I was on the cruise, I saw you with all those women. Even though I knew it was your job to play host, I still couldn't help but wonder whether you weren't just stringing me along," she added.

"Well, I don't know if I should thank you for being honest, or not. I think the bottom line here is how we feel about each other and if we can overcome the hurt we've inflicted on one another," he said simply.

"I'm willing to try, if you are," Mel said immediately.

"Are you sure?" he asked with penetrating eyes. "I still have a few cruises to go, and there will be plenty of women around me. Will you be able to trust me?"

"I don't know what you're getting at."

"Are you still going to doubt me?" he asked.

"Jim, I think we should decide what kind of relationship we have before you ask me a question like that," she stated with determination.

"Well, I'm talking about us having a future together."

"You mean, getting married?" she asked.

The minute the words were out of her mouth, she wondered how she had managed to be so brave, asking the one question whose right answer meant the world to her.

"Yes, if that's what you want," he returned.

"What about you?" she asked with raised brows. "It takes two to tango, you know. I don't mean to be so abrupt, but I think we're beating around the bush here. Did you just ask me to marry you, or was I only dreaming?"

Jim laughed, the sound was music to her heart. "Yes, I'm asking you to marry me, you idiot. Will you be my wife, Melanie?"

Mel stared at him in disbelief. "I don't believe this," she exclaimed. "I think someone should pinch me."

"Come over here, and I'll pinch you," Jim replied playfully.

She looked into his bright, eager eyes and smiled. Instantly, she wanted to be in his arms. The minute she reached him, he wrapped his strong arms around her.

Pinching her arm lightly, he asked, "Well, what do you say? How do you feel about being Mrs. James O'Dowd?"

Mel smiled brightly. "I think it feels wonderful!"

Jim's eyes misted. "Oh, darling, you've made me so happy!"

His lips swooped down to hers, his kiss warm and filled with need as his eager tongue parted her lips and probed shamelessly. His desire thrilled her beyond belief, and she matched his passion as she kissed him with her whole being.

Gently he eased her down onto the bed, his lips locked against hers. His hand moved under her dress to skim her hips and thighs, and her body shuddered with delight. His touch was divine ecstasy, and a fire spread to her heart. She was with the man she would spend the rest of her life with, and she suddenly understood the true meaning of happiness.

Taking her hand, he guided her to touch him. She stroked him gently, then more aggressively, aware of his deep moans as his passion mounted. As he cried out with release, her heart filled with joy at having pleased the man she loved.

"That was beautiful. Thank you, darling," he whispered with contented eyes.

"The pleasure was all mine," she answered in a husky voice.

Urgently he undressed her and then stared down at her silken, aroused body. She was touched by the heart-rending tenderness of his gaze, and the need to experience him overcame her as she couldn't believe this wonderful man would soon be her husband.

His hand cupped her breast as his tongue explored its rosy peak, rousing a melting sweetness through her.

Suddenly nothing else mattered except to be a part of this man, to feel his strength and vitality surge within her, and to become one. Her nails dug into his back, urging him to take her. Immediately he responded to her unspoken plea, and with one expert thrust, her heart exploded with all the pent-up emotions that she had saved for the man who had become dearer than life to her.

Their love drove them into a maddening frenzy, carrying them off on a velvet cloud as their bodies responded in exquisite harmony. Never had she given herself so freely, so completely, and all barriers magically slipped away and were replaced by trust and caring. Suddenly their passion exploded, then was released, and the world was stilled as a deep feeling of peace covered Mel as she lay wrapped in her lover's arms.

Later that evening, they ate ravenously and then decided to do some dancing. Seated in the modern discothèque, they listened to a lively band.

Holding her hand, he murmured, "We'll have to make sure that we book a cruise to celebrate our fiftieth wedding anniversary."

Mel laughed and said, "You've got a deal!"

"I love you, Melanie."

"I love you, too."

He flashed her one of the most beautiful smiles that she had ever seen, and it touched her heart and warmed her soul. He was all that she needed in the world, and she felt whole.

"Helen wants to be maid of honor," she said with a grin.

He shot her a skeptical glance. "You were pretty sure of yourself, weren't you?"

She giggled. "I wasn't, but Helen was."

"Well, I'm glad someone talked you into coming after me," he said.

"How do you know that someone had to talk me into it?" she asked.

"Knowing you, with that stubborn streak of yours, I would have had to come after you," he answered. "I would have come, too, Melanie, I just needed to sort some things out."

"I'm glad you told me that."

"The minute I knew that I didn't want to live my life without you, I knew that I was hooked," he said quietly.

"Jim, I hope being with me doesn't make you feel hooked," she said.

"Only a figure of speech, darling," he returned, reaching over and pulling her close to him.

She smiled as a woman's melodious voice was heard accompanying the music. She glanced in the direction of the sound, and to her surprise, she recognized the singer. It was the same blonde who had given Jim her number.

Mel immediately turned back to Jim and gave him a dirty look.

He chuckled. "She wanted a job, but how could I tell you that?"

"Oh, Jim, I don't know what I'm going to do with you," she remarked, shaking her head.

"You're going to kiss me and be my wife," he stated happily.

"I think you're right," she returned as she snuggled against him and kissed him.